"Someone's following us," Sable screamed.

"Just keep driving, and get your headlights on or we'll plunge into the canal," Murph replied.

Sable complied, downshifting for a burst of power, bracing herself for the dangerous turn at the edge of the deep, water-filled channel less than a quarter mile ahead.

Despite her speed, the car behind drew closer. She tightened her grip on the steering wheel.

High beams swung around the curve and into her face. Swerving, Sable realized too late how close she was to the canal. She yanked the steering wheel hard left. The road was too slick. The Camaro slammed against a concrete abutment.

"We're going over!" Murph grabbed Sable's arm. "Jump!"

Books by Hannah Alexander

Love Inspired Suspense

Note of Peril #1
Under Suspicion #25
Death Benefits #60
Hidden Motive #95

Love Inspired Historical

Hideaway Home #3

Steeple Hill Single Title

Hideaway
Safe Haven
Last Resort
Fair Warning
Grave Risk

HANNAH ALEXANDER

is the pseudonym of husband-and-wife writing team Cheryl and Mel Hodde (pronounced "Hoddee"). When they first met, Mel had just begun his new job as an E.R. doctor in Cheryl's hometown, and Cheryl was working on a novel. Cheryl's matchmaking pastor set them up on an unexpected blind date at a local restaurant. Surprised by the sneak attack, Cheryl blurted the first thing that occurred to her: "You're a doctor? Could you help me paralyze someone?" Mel was shocked. "Only temporarily, of course," she explained when she saw his expression. "And only fictitiously. I'm writing a novel."

They began brainstorming immediately. Eighteen months later they were married, and the novels they set in fictitious Ozark towns began to sell. The first novel in the Hideaway series, published in the Steeple Hill Single Title program, won the prestigious Christy Award for Best Romance in 2004.

HANNAH ALEXANDER

Hidden Motive

Steeple
Hill®

Published by Steeple Hill Books™

STEEPLE HILL BOOKS

Steeple
Hill®

ISBN-13: 978-0-373-44285-0
ISBN-10:   0-373-44285-8

HIDDEN MOTIVE

Printed in U.S.A.

The LORD is my light and my salvation—
whom shall I fear? The LORD is the stronghold
of my life—of whom shall I be afraid?
—*Psalms* 27:1

To Randy and Jason, always beloved.
Thanks for the memories.

ONE

Dr. Sable Chamberlin had begun to detest her telephone's ring tone. Not only did she hate the harsh sound, but the ring often summoned her to the Boswell Community Hospital for an emergency. Being on call sixty hours a week had gotten old. She wasn't on call this evening, however; she was in mourning.

She slid the cordless receiver from the stand on the counter and pressed the answer button, glancing through her kitchen window at the lightning over the company town of Freemont, Oklahoma. It seemed much later than six o'clock on this February evening.

"Sable, that you?" The voice of her elderly friend, Noah Erwin, held comfort.

"Hi, Noah."

"How'd the funeral go?"

She closed her eyes, tears still close. Her grandfather, Josiah Kessinger, had been the reason for her move to Freemont from her home in the Missouri Ozarks.

"It went, Noah."

"Hard, huh?"

"Especially the accusations against him."

"All false," Noah said.

"I know." Her grandfather's death on Monday had coincided with a rumor of fraud. Sable had also been implicated in the alleged deception. Since she and her grandfather weren't natives of this tightly knit mining community, they made easy targets, it seemed.

"You just get back to town?" Noah asked.

"Yes, I have a shift tomorrow." Saturday was a busy day at the clinic. "What's up?"

"I have a package that was sent to you in care of my address. I'd bring it to you, but my truck's in for repairs."

"From whom?"

"Josiah."

"Grandpa?"

"It's his writing. No name on the return address, but it's stamped Eagle Rock, Missouri."

"Would you open it, please?" Sable asked. "If it's something important, I'll drive out."

She heard a ripping sound. Noah said something under his breath, and then paused. The pause became a protracted silence.

"Noah?"

"Lord help us all," he murmured.

"What?"

Noah continued to mutter as paper rustled. Sable didn't rush him. He'd been her patient since her second day on the job at the Freemont clinic. He'd also become the most important influence in her life here. Because of Noah, she and Grandpa had found hope for the future—and a whole new reason for living.

"Sable, you'd better come on out," Noah said at last. "Something's up. I knew Josiah had a lot on his mind, but the old rascal never was much for sharing his thoughts."

"What is it?"

"You should see the stuff he's dug up," Noah said. "Papers and letters about dirty deals, pictures, reports."

"Dirty deals? What kind of—"

"You might think about packing your bags and heading back to Missouri," Noah said. "Here's one of those sticky notes. Says these are copies. Originals in Missouri. You got any idea where—" He broke off.

"Noah?"

"Thought I heard something."

"Like what?" This felt increasingly bad.

"Probably the wind. Just get out here, okay? Josiah hinted about spies amongst us, and—" He broke off again. "What was that noise?" Silence, then, distantly, "Hello? Who's there?"

She gripped the receiver and took a slow, steady breath. *Just the wind.*

Noah came back on the line. "Sorry about that. I'm a little jumpy is all."

"I'll call the police."

"No! These notes suggest someone in the sheriff's office is dirty. Murph's got his cell phone on him. I'll call him out, just to be safe."

Paul Murphy, a paramedic at the clinic, was solid and strong. Sable liked and trusted the man.

"I'll be waiting on the porch," Noah said. "See you in about ten."

She grabbed her car keys and billfold from the kitchen counter and pulled on her coat. Noah lived alone in an old farmhouse four miles from town. She rushed outside, locking the door behind her. Instinctively, as she hurried to the car, her hand went up to the old pocket watch she wore on a chain around her neck, an unexpected Christmas gift from her grandfather.

Ever since he'd given her the watch, he'd become more and more secretive. Three weeks ago, he'd told her, "Darlin', if anything happens to me, get out of Oklahoma. Don't look back. This isn't any kind of town for a young lady like you."

Recalling those words, she jumped into her Camaro and backed from the driveway. Soon, maybe she would have more pieces of this puzzle. She hoped they didn't raise more questions.

A flash of lightning illuminated Noah Erwin's sprawling old house. The violent, approaching storm lit the sky, accentuating the darkness in the house. Noah wasn't on the porch waiting for her, as he'd said he would be.

She unlatched the gate, pulled it open with a creak of rusty hinges, and then stepped carefully along the flagstone path. She stopped as another flash of lightning lit the porch and the wide-open doorway.

In that instant, Sable was blasted with shock at the sight of her elderly friend sprawled across the threshold, his body pinned between the door frame and both the heavy oak and screen doors.

With a cry, Sable rushed up the porch steps and fell to her knees at her friend's side. "Noah! Oh, Lord, no!"

More lightning illuminated a pool of blood from a hole in Noah's temple. His glazed eyes held the blank stare of death.

Anguished beyond thought, she felt for a pulse at his throat. Noah's head fell sideways, exposing a mass of blood at the back of his skull. The shooter had completed the job.

Sable felt the porch spin. Numb with shock, she leaned against the door frame as tears blinded her and icy wind whipped her hair across her face.

This was murder. She dashed the tears from her eyes and the hair from her face and cast a frantic look around the shadowed entryway and the living room beyond. Dark shapes lurked in every corner of the huge room. Another flash of lightning cast the sofa and chairs and Noah's old desk in sharp relief.

The storm blocked any other sounds and the wind scattered papers across the foyer. These papers…were those the ones Noah had called her about? Terrified of lingering, yet desperate to find out why he had died, she grabbed all the sheets she could find and stuffed them into a pocket of her coat.

The wind broke briefly, and Sable heard a footfall in the darkness near the kitchen door.

Movement! Lightning revealed a man lunging from the shadows. Sable screamed and stumbled backward, tripping over Noah's body. She fell on her side, then scrambled up and away.

The man grabbed her coat sleeve. She screamed again, yanking from his grip, running off the porch toward her car.

Footsteps pounded behind her, splashing mud. She'd never make the car. She broke away and dove into a clump of bushes.

Thorns scraped her hands. She charged through the hedgerow, fighting brambles that clung to her clothes.

Sable fumbled in her pocket for her keys, setting her sights on her car, but her foot caught on a root and she fell. The man grabbed her. She swung around to claw at his face...there was no face.

Lightning revealed a ski mask.

A brilliant flash of headlights pierced through the spiny branches of the shrubs. The attacker released her abruptly, swung away, stumbled, broke back through the hedgerow and disappeared into the darkness.

Sable froze, heart pounding, breath coming in hard rasps. The vehicle passed a large SUV. She turned and ran toward her car, but the SUV pulled in behind it, blocking her escape. She plunged into the blackness beyond the driveway.

"Hey!" a man shouted from the vehicle.

Sable staggered over the uneven ground. Again she heard the sound of pursuing footsteps. She reached level ground and raced toward the toolshed. There might be a weapon among the garden tools, maybe a hoe, or—

Large, strong hands gripped her shoulders and spun her around, shoving her against the wall of the shed.

She screamed, jerking her knee upward, connecting with something solid.

The man grunted, but held fast.

She raked her nails down the side of his neck, kicked at his legs. "Let go of me!"

Another grunt. "Dr. Chamberlin?" Shocked surprise.

"Get away from me!"

"Sable!" He grabbed her by the arms. "Doctor, stop it!"

The familiar voice registered. She froze, recognizing the light scent of aftershave, the breadth of his shoulders.

"Doctor, it's me. It's Murph." He groaned in pain.

Relief flooded her, followed by a rising alarm at her frantic resistance. "Murph?" She peered through the shadowy gloom at the face of Paul Murphy—the paramedic who had been with the clinic for the past six weeks.

"Oh, Murph, I'm so—"

"What happened? Where's Noah?"

She swallowed hard as the first fat drops of rain splashed against her face. "He's on the porch. Oh, Murph, he's dead!"

There was a deep gasp.

"He's been murdered." She fought back her own horror. No time. "He called me no more than fifteen minutes ago with—"

Murph released her and turned toward the house, sucking in air as if he'd been kicked. "He called me, too."

Sable grabbed his arm. "Murph, don't go up there. He was shot. That had to be his murderer you saw chasing me. That murderer is armed."

Murph looked back at her. "All I saw was you running."

"Your headlights startled him and he ran, but I don't know how far. He could be anywhere and he has a gun. We've got to get away."

There was a loud crackle of thunder, and when the echo died away, Sable heard an approaching siren.

She caught Murph's arm. "That's got to be the police, and Noah warned me not to trust them. We've got to go *now*. Murph, come on." She released him and raced toward her car. "Get in!"

The siren grew louder as Sable jumped into the car, slammed the door and turned on the key. The motor sprang to life with a rumble. As she put the car into gear, Murph slid in on the passenger side.

The wide tires of the Camaro tore up grass and slung mud. Sable held her breath and pressed the accelerator to the floorboard. The car cleared the bushes at the far end of Noah's front yard just as red flashing lights stained the night sky. Sable didn't switch on her headlights.

She turned onto a straight stretch of road. "So you believe me?"

"Yes. Are you okay? Did that man hurt you?"

"He killed Noah!" She fought tears.

Her ruse with the headlights worked. As the sirens receded, she relaxed her foot on the accelerator, but too soon. Lights hit her rearview mirror. No colors, no siren.

"Someone's following us," she told Murph.

"Just keep driving and get your headlights on or we'll plunge into the canal."

Sable complied, downshifting for a burst of power, bracing herself for the dangerous turn at the edge of the deep, water-filled channel less than a quarter mile ahead.

Despite her speed, the car behind drew closer. She tightened her grip on the steering wheel.

Only a few hundred feet from the curve, the other car accelerated. Sable pressed her right foot to the floorboard and the Camaro responded with another burst of speed.

High beams swung around the curve ahead and into her face. Swerving, Sable realized too late how close she was to the canal. She yanked the steering wheel hard left. The road was too slick. The Camaro slammed against a concrete abutment. Murph's door flew open. Sable screamed.

"We're going over!" Murph grabbed Sable's arm. "Jump!"

Sable dived across the seat toward the open door. The car careened off the blacktop and plummeted toward the water.

Pushing free from the car, Sable and Murph plunged into the icy wet blackness.

TWO

Paul Murphy broke surface, gasping for air in the numbing cold. Waves from the car's impact washed over him and he fought to stay afloat. He strained through the darkness for a sign of Dr. Chamberlin, but before he could call out, two sets of headlights penetrated the darkness from above.

Hampered by his down coat, Murph swam to the bank of the canal. He grasped the branches of a bush above his head, and pulled himself from the water. He started to call out, but he heard car doors closing.

In the wash of the headlights, he caught the outline of a dark form about ten feet to his right. Dr. Chamberlin. Sable. Now if only she would remain still until—

Male voices rat-a-tatted across the water's surface.

"Who was it? Did you see?"

"Had to be Chamberlin. It was her car."

"I know that," the first man snapped. "Who was with her?"

"Some big guy."

"There was a Bronco in the driveway. We'll have McCann run the license plate." The beam of a flashlight traveled slowly over the surface of the water. Murph didn't move.

"Anything out there?"

"Not yet. What brought you out?" The beam continued its search.

"Heard some rumors."

"From that tap at the old man's house?"

There was a grunt. "Kessinger was on to more than we realized."

"Sounds that way. We've got to keep the Feds out of it. We need that package Kessinger mailed."

"If Chamberlin was at the house, she had to've gotten it."

"Then it's somewhere in this canal. We find her body, or the car, and we'll have what we need."

A new voice joined in. "Hey! I just got the call. Somebody shot the old guy."

The flashlight beam stopped sweeping the water, redirected to the roadway above. Peering up the embankment, Murph saw three dark figures huddled together. The men's voices lowered as the conversation continued.

"Noah Erwin," the newcomer said softly. "Got him in the head."

There was a short pause, and Murph frowned, confused. If these guys hadn't killed Noah, then who had? Were there two factions at work? How big *was* this operation?

"Won't have to worry about that one, then," said one of the men.

Murph gritted his teeth at the dismissive attitude, as if Noah was something to be dumped on a garbage heap.

"So Chamberlin shot the old fool, took the evidence and tried to get away."

"Some friend she turned out to be."

"The chief's gotta be thrilled about this one," the speaker said drily.

Murph shivered in the icy air as the conversation ceased and the flashlight beam played across the water again. Sable was no longer visible.

The beam of the flashlight began to edge toward him. He closed his eyes, willing himself to stillness. Seconds later, he heard a scuffle of footsteps.

"Get the car out of the canal," came a terse command.

"Tomorrow we'll release the news that the fleeing killers paid for the murder with their lives."

The light retreated, voices fading as the men walked away. When Murph heard the revving of engines, he rushed back down the steep embankment toward the spot he had last seen Sable. In the blackness of the night, he could see little; the storm had passed, taking the lightning.

Water surged directly beside him; Sable shot from the inky blackness of the canal. She gasped and choked as she struggled toward the bank.

Murph grabbed her arms and pulled her from the water.

"Are they gone?" she asked between gasps.

"They're gone." He drew her close for warmth.

"I had nowhere to hide," she said. "The flashlight beam was about to reach me. I had to go under, but it was so cold."

Her teeth began to chatter. Her breath misted the air. "I held my breath as long as I could, but the c-current k-k-kept—"

"We've got to warm you up or you'll get hypothermia." Murph helped her climb to safety on the steep bank. "Are you okay?"

"Freezing," she said with a shudder. "I'm f-freezing."

He opened his coat and drew her against him, wrapping her as completely as he could away from the wind. "You heard?"

"M-most of it, until I went under."

Awkwardly, attempting to keep them both enclosed within the protective folds of his wet coat, Murph helped Sable along the bank to a muddy track.

"We've got to get out of here," Murph said grimly. "I'm going with you to Missouri."

Sable stiffened, her teeth still chattering. "How?"

"We can take a bus from Freemont," Murph said. "Right now they think we're dead. We want them to keep thinking that, at least until we're away from this place."

"D-didn't you m-move here from Wichita?" Her voice rose and fell as her whole body shook. "Give y-yourself a break and get out of this mess. You're not a p-part—"

"I'm part of it now," he said. "And stop trying to talk. You need to focus on warming up."

"Medically speaking, wh-whether or not a patient talks—"

"Dr. Chamberlin, be quiet."

"L-look, I ap-p-ppreciate everything y-you're—"

"You're in no position to argue with me right now," he said, pulling the coat more tightly around her. He *had* to go with her, whether she invited him or not.

"Do you have any money?" Sable asked. "I have an ATM—"

"We can't use credit or ATM cards. They can be tracked."

"You don't think we could be tracked if we take a bus?" she challenged.

"Unless you want to steal a car, we don't have a choice. We can only hope they continue to believe we're dead in the canal. I have cash in the lining of my coat for emergencies." He didn't tell her about the gun.

She looked up at him. "Why are you prepared for an emergency?"

"I'm always prepared. Let's just get to Missouri."

THREE

In the early hours of Saturday morning, the Southwestern Missouri weather, known for its February fickleness, was oppressively bleak in the Ozarks. The thick layer of clouds had pursued Sable and Murph from Freemont, hovering at each stopover, threatening further delays.

Sable leaned back. She couldn't sleep, but if she could close her eyes for a few moments...

They had reached Joplin late last night, where the layover stretched two extra hours due to a storm in Kansas, which had delayed their connecting bus. Murph had made a futile attempt to rent a car while Sable had watched the doors at the station, expecting either Noah's killers or the police.

When they'd finally boarded this bus at 3:30 a.m., Sable had been jumpy with paranoia, suspiciously studying the four other passengers, including a teenage boy and a gray-haired lady.

By the time they reached Cassville, near the Missouri-Arkansas border, the temperature took another plunge, freezing rain on the windshield. These conditions could be dangerous.

Sable looked out on the wilderness of the Mark Twain National Forest as the bus lumbered around the curves of Highway 86. The engine muffled the sound of rainfall. The methodic swish of the wipers was hypnotic....

The driver's alarmed grunt startled Sable. The redheaded woman worked the steering wheel, her muscular arms taut with tension. The roads had quickly become opaque with ice.

Jerri, the driver, had held conversations with everyone on the bus. She was a good tour guide, but her driving skills stank.

Sable straightened in her seat. "We're getting close," she told Murph. "Only a couple more miles." She wasn't aware of her tightly clenched hands until Murph touched them.

"It won't help to try to drive the bus for her." His steady baritone held reassurance.

In fact, Paul Murphy had been a calming influence since the day she'd met him—a good quality in a paramedic, and especially good right now.

"I'll feel better once we're off the road," she said.

Murph nodded. "Apparently, this storm didn't show up on the weather reports or we'd still be stranded in Joplin."

"Happens a lot in this area," Sable said. "I just hope the rain stops soon, because we'll have to walk to my family's house."

"There's no one who can pick us up?"

She shook her head. "I tried calling and got the answering machine. One of my brothers lives in Eureka Springs, Arkansas. My mother was planning to stay with him for a while after my grandfather's funeral."

Fortunately, Sable had been able to persuade Jerri to let them off at the end of the quarter-mile drive to the farmhouse when they reached their destination.

"My father died when I was sixteen," Sable told Murph. "Mom moved with me and my two brothers back here to my grandfather's place and this has been home ever since." She instinctively grasped the pocket watch that dangled from a chain around her neck. Sadness overwhelmed her.

"You wear that all the time," Murph observed.

"Grandpa gave it to me this Christmas. When I was little, I loved to sit on his lap, wind this watch, and listen to it tick. It doesn't tick anymore, but I still have the memories."

"Hold tightly to those," Murph said.

She looked up at him, her gaze drawn to the red welts on his neck. "I'm so sorry, Murph. I feel awful about—"

"That's your fourth and final apology." He touched the

scratches. "You have a few self-defense tricks, but I could show you more effective techniques, if you promise not to use them on me."

"Just identify yourself before I strike." She kept her voice soft. "Do you think anyone else here—" she nodded toward the others on the bus "—hails from Freemont?"

"I don't know, but I admit I'll be relieved when we make it to the house," he said.

"Me too, but you heard that conversation at the canal last night." She lowered her voice, gave a quick glance around the bus. "Those men will know where to look for me, don't you think?"

"Don't borrow trouble."

"I won't borrow it, but I want to be prepared." She glanced out the window. "If only I knew more." She had lost the papers she'd gathered at Noah's house when she'd plunged into the canal.

"I wish we hadn't been forced to leave Noah's body the way we did," she said, still feeling the shock of his murder.

Murph nodded, silent. She couldn't miss the taut jaw and flaring of nostrils—suppressed emotion.

"You and Noah really took to each other, didn't you?"

Murph paused. "He was special." He looked at Sable. "He did not believe your grandfather was guilty of fraud."

"He talked to you about that?"

"This past week everyone's been talking about it."

"Noah was right," she said. "Grandpa wouldn't have defrauded his friends. It's true that he'd been in debt for years, but he was almost solvent again when he died."

The bus slid. Sable's hand closed around Murph's forearm. After an uncertain moment, the bus glided to a stop at the road's edge. Sable released her grip on Murph. Another mile or so, and they would be off this bus. She'd rather walk in the freezing rain than risk an accident on the cliffs up ahead.

"Josiah wasn't a prospector, was he?" Murph asked softly as the bus driver eased her foot from the brake.

Sable glance at Murph. She knew he was only trying to

distract her from the road, but she'd overheard several comments around Freemont about Grandpa's intentions when he went into debt again to purchase the Seitz mine.

"He didn't salt that mine," she said. "He and Noah were misinformed about the layout of the land before they purchased it. They should have checked it out, but they didn't plant ore in it later to save their necks."

"Didn't their third partner have some input?"

"That would be Otis Boswell. Our *employer,*" she stressed. "The man practically owns Freemont, so why pull a shoddy deal like that for a few more bucks?"

"How well do you know him?" Murph asked.

Sable shrugged. "He once lived here in Missouri. His land adjoined ours. He and Grandpa hunted together sometimes. They weren't great friends, but Grandpa never turned down a hunting trip." Her voice caught. She felt lost and vulnerable.

Murph gently patted her hand.

"Why did you come with me?" Sable asked.

For a moment, he didn't reply, and again she saw the tautening of his expression, that quiet caution.

"I couldn't let you try to get here by yourself," he said. "What if you'd been followed?"

"You've known me, what, six weeks? Why didn't you run?"

"They'll be after both of us once they discover we didn't die in that canal. We're safer together than apart." He glanced out the window. "How is your family home set up for security?"

"It isn't," she said. "We've never had need for it, but the house is built over the mouth of a cave. It could serve as a hideaway if necessary."

"At the station, you told me about some evidence your grandpa gathered. Evidence about what? About whom?"

"Good question."

"Wouldn't he have left something like that in a bank safe-deposit box?"

"Not necessarily. He often returned home on the weekends, and if he had documents of any kind, he would've brought them."

"So they'd be in the house somewhere."

"Maybe. There's an old safe upstairs in the attic, but no one except Grandpa knew the combination. He could be very secretive about some subjects." Her dear, stubborn grandfather.

"We have to find out what happened," Murph said.

She glanced outside, studied the landmarks, and then got to her feet. "I'd better go tell the driver we're getting close."

Murph pulled their coats from the overhead compartment and followed Sable to the front. Four rows up, a chubby man the driver had called Perry Chadwick snored softly, his arm flung out in front of him.

The bus lurched and Sable grabbed the seat beside her, earning a glare from the hard-muscled man who sat there. Simmons was his name, if she remembered correctly.

With a quick apology, Sable and Murph continued forward.

The driver glanced into the wide rearview mirror as they approached. "It's getting worse. Better sit down."

Sable took a place beside the elderly woman seated behind the bus driver. "Jerri, you can drop us off just around the next curve, past the speed limit sign."

The driver nodded.

Sable's seatmate flashed a smile. "You're getting off at the old Kessinger Cave?"

"You know of it?" Sable asked.

"Who doesn't? I lived in the area years ago." She held her hand out. "I'm Audry Hawkins, and—"

The bus lurched sideways in a long, icy glide. The darkened tree line swept nearer in a smooth arc. Sable knew the ground dropped steeply here. She held her breath as the bus slid toward the precipice with almost casual grace.

Jerri's face was white as she wrestled the steering wheel and pumped the brake. The bus slowly straightened, once more parallel with the center line when it came to a stop.

Again, Sable thought about the cliffs ahead. The next time the bus lost traction, the result might not be so fortunate.

"If there was another way to get where I'm going," Audry murmured softly, "I'd have taken it."

"What is your destination?" Sable asked.

"My great-nephew is getting married in Eureka Springs," Audry said. "Thorncrown Chapel. His bride wanted to be married on Valentine's Day." She shook her head and murmured under her breath, "Far be it from me to question the girl's judgment. I'm just the elderly great-aunt."

The muscle-bound man with the steel gaze—Simmons— came down the aisle. "In case you hadn't noticed," he said to the bus driver in a gravelly voice, "this road is dangerous. If they're getting off here, so am I."

"Agreed," came the high-pitched, nervous voice of the chubby man behind them. "I don't relish plunging to an early death in these hills. Couldn't we park until this blows over?"

Jerri shook her head. "Do you folks really want to camp out here for two or three days? It could take that long before the road is cleared. I have a responsibility to get my passengers to their destinations, and—"

"Alive," Simmons snapped. "Doesn't your license say anything about that?" He peered at the photo ID displayed at the front of the bus, then muttered a curse. "That's not your license up there. It isn't your picture. What's going on here?"

"The driver who was scheduled for this run called in sick," Jerri explained. "I'm the last-minute substitution."

"Have you driven this route before?" the chubby man asked.

Jerri hesitated, then said, "It's a new route for me."

"You don't know the route?" Audry Hawkins exclaimed.

The chubby man groaned. "I didn't need to know that."

"Let me get this straight," Simmons growled. "It's raining sleet, we've got a road that bends like a pretzel, and a clueless driver. There's not another car on this road, unless you count the pickup in the ditch."

Sable cleared her throat and spoke into the tense silence. "Perhaps we *should* stop for a while." She didn't want to do this, but what other choice was there? "I know this road. I've seen cars that have plunged off the cliffs up ahead."

"But we can't just pull over and stop, with nowhere to go," Jerri said.

Sable closed her eyes and said a quick prayer. A few months ago, she might have allowed the bus to continue on and hope for the best, but now—due to Noah's influence—she knew she couldn't let it happen.

"Our drop-off place is only a couple hundred feet ahead," she said, "before the cliffs. You can't tackle the cliffs on this ice." Sable hesitated, then gave in to the inevitable. "There's room at the house for everyone." She wouldn't be able to live with herself if five people plunged to their deaths because she was trying to save her own life.

FOUR

Paul Murphy had long ago learned to cover his alarm with a look of calm detachment. It would be criminal, of course, to allow the bus to continue on this impossible road; he knew the invitation Sable issued was necessary.

"Are you sure about this?" the driver asked Sable. "No telling how long we'll be stuck here if we stop now."

Perry Chadwick cleared his throat, his triple chins jiggling. "I would prefer to stay here indefinitely if the alternative is to plunge off a cliff. I vote we stay."

"No voting to it," Simmons growled. "We're staying."

Murph studied the two men. If someone knew he and Sable were alive and had taken the bus from Freemont, it would have been easy to follow them to Joplin, buy a ticket and join them. It also concerned him that even Jerri, the bus driver, had been a sudden replacement.

All the other passengers had arrived at the Joplin bus station long after he and Sable. What better way to find the secluded Kessinger place—and the evidence stored there—than to tail Josiah Kessinger's granddaughter?

On the other hand, the men at the canal had seemed convinced that he and Sable had gone down with the car.

The older lady, Audry Hawkins, reached forward and patted the driver's shoulder. "This highway is treacherous in bad weather, especially if you aren't familiar with it. Let us go to Sable's house before the road or the driveway collect more ice."

Sable gestured to the mailbox spotlighted by the bus headlights. Beside it, a narrow drive curved down between leafless trees and green cedars. "You can pull over there, Jerri. We'll have to walk from here."

"Walk?" Perry Chadwick's voice rose to a squeak, his jowly face quivering in alarm as Jerri maneuvered the big vehicle forward. "In this weather? How far?"

"It's a little over a quarter of a mile," Sable said.

"Why can't we drive there?" the portly man protested.

"The bus won't fit, you moron," Simmons snapped.

Jerri parked the bus at the edge of the road. "Okay, folks, we're parked, but let's stay here on the bus, where it's dry, until the sun comes up in a few hours. I don't relish walking anywhere in the dark on that ice."

"I'm sorry," Audry said, "but speaking from experience, I intend to go now. I recently lost a dear friend who fell and broke her hip and didn't survive the surgery. The longer we wait here, the thicker the ground ice and the slicker the walk. Sable obviously knows this drive, and I have no doubt she can guide us safely to her home."

For a moment, everyone hesitated.

Simmons got up and retrieved a duffel bag from beneath his seat. "The gal's right—that ice isn't melting. Let's get this over with."

A muttered query came from the center of the bus. A shaggy-haired teenage boy poked his head over the seat and peered at them with sleepy brown eyes. "Are we there?"

"No, I'm sorry, Bryce." Jerri set the hand brake and unbuckled her seat belt. "Get your coat and umbrella, if you have one." She explained what they were doing.

"In the dark?" Bryce protested. "In the rain?"

"In the *freezing* rain," Perry stressed.

"That's right." Jerri scanned the tiny group, and her gaze fell on Murph. "Mr. Murphy, please check the overhead compartment in the back for umbrellas and the flashlight."

"I have my little one." Audry pulled a penlight from her purse and showed it to the others. "Amazing what a little beam can do in the darkness. I wouldn't be without it."

"Better save it," Jerri said. "We might need the light later. Everybody gather your things while I try to call dispatch."

Five minutes later, after Jerri had tried the radio and a cell phone to no avail, everyone realized they would be out of touch with the world, here in the hills.

"We can try to make contact again when we get to the house," Sable said. "The sooner we get there, the more likely that the telephone lines haven't broken yet."

Perry returned to the front wearing a long coat, pulling a hard-sided case with wheels and a telescoping handle. "I can't believe we're doing this. Did you see those tree limbs? The ice must be an inch thick already."

"Your complaints aren't helping," Jerri snapped. "Carry only the bare essentials, an overnight case if you must, but no more." She indicated his suitcase. "That's too much."

Perry arched a pale eyebrow, surprisingly resolute. "This goes where I go."

Jerri flicked off the bus lights and turned on her flashlight. "Be careful and stay together, everybody." She pulled the door open to a maelstrom of wind and ice.

Murph stepped out first, catching his breath as the rain pelted his face and neck, slapping softly against the hardening surface of the ground. He stomped into a pile of ice-coated leaves and found traction…of sorts.

"Watch your footing," he told the others. "It's treacherous." He turned to help Sable.

She hesitated before taking his hand. He could see the anxiety in her eyes.

"Come on, keep it moving," Simmons snapped behind her.

Evading Murph's outstretched hand, the muscular man with the gravel voice landed on the ground with surprising agility.

Perry Chadwick came next. When Murph reached up to help

him with his suitcase, he jerked it back. "Important equipment," he murmured, allowing Murph to steady him as he stepped down.

When they'd all gathered beneath a clump of cedar trees, sheltered from the worst of the rain, they opened their umbrellas. Except for Jerri's flashlight, the frigid darkness was absolute.

Murph couldn't help thinking this predawn experience was comparable to the ordeal he and Sable had gone through the night before. How much more would they have to endure?

As Sable scrambled for traction along the dark drive, icy needles of rain stung her face, whipped by the wind beneath the protection of the umbrella.

She cast a sideways glance at Murph, whose footing seemed secure and steady. In contrast, Perry Chadwick dragged his case behind him, stumbling and sliding with every step. By the time the group had reached the cliffs, a couple hundred feet from the highway, he was puffing and gasping for breath.

The road dipped at a sharp angle, hugging the hillside in a hairpin curve that overlooked a ravine. A sudden gust of wind blasted Sable with cold sleet, attacking her umbrella, nearly jerking it from her grip. Audry cried out. Perry slid to his knees.

Losing traction, Sable instinctively reached for Murph's arm.

He caught and steadied her. "Are you okay?"

"Yes, but it's getting worse. This ice is almost impossible." She raised her voice to be heard by the others. "Everyone stay as close as possible to the hillside here. And take your time. You don't want to lose your footing now."

They had walked only a few more yards along the road when Perry gave a startled grunt and stumbled against Jerri, knocking the flashlight from her grip. It clattered to the ground, and in a spiral of rotating rays, slid over the edge of the cliff into empty, black space. With everyone shocked into silence, the spatter of rain was so loud, they didn't hear the flashlight hit bottom. The darkness engulfed them.

"You idiot!" Simmons snapped.

"Oh, no," Perry said, "I'm so sorry. What are we—"

"Everybody stay put!" Jerri shouted from ahead of them. "Audry, where's your penlight?"

"It's right here," Audry said. "Would someone please help me hold my umbrella for a moment?"

Murph released Sable and stepped backward just as someone else—the teenager Bryce? The chubby Perry Chadwick?—cried out and fell.

In the blackness, the wind attacked Sable's umbrella again, wrenching it from her grasp. Then someone shoved her from the right. Hard.

She screamed, flinging out her arms out as her feet flew out from under her. Her shoulder slammed against the ice-packed drive. Her slide gained momentum.

She screamed again, grasping desperately for a tree, a bush, anything in the darkness that would stop her descent to the ravine. Rocks gouged at her, but offered no handhold.

"Help me!" she cried as she neared the cliff's edge.

"Sable, grab my hand!" Murph shouted.

She reached up blindly through the darkness, but her body rammed against a boulder, knocking the breath from her lungs, stunning her. She tumbled sideways. Her arm smacked against something. She grabbed a sapling that halted her slide with a wrenching jolt as her left foot kicked out into open air.

She tried to gain traction with her right foot, tried to dig the toes of her shoe into the earth to gain a foothold, but she could not climb up. She heard the scatter of rocks and debris tumble into the ravine.

"Sable!" Murph called down from above. "Grab something!"

"I...I have," she said. "But I can't hold on much longer!" As she began to lose her grasp on the sapling, she reached up with her left hand and tried to reinforce her grip, kicking frantically against the ground.

The sapling bent, then snapped. She screamed as she fell.

"Sable!" Murph shouted.

She landed hard on her back on a narrow ledge. Digging her fingers into the rocky earth, she paused to catch her breath.

"I'm here," she tried to call, her voice barely more than a whisper. "Murph, I'm here!" But for how long? How could she climb back up to the others?

FIVE

The rocky ledge gouged into Sable's back as rain slapped her face. She was going to die.

"Sable, hold on!" Murph's voice came from far above her. "I'm coming down."

"No!" she called. "There's rope at the house. If you could just get there and..." But how could she hold on that long? Her hands were already growing numb.

A small light flickered from above, and Audry called out, "Hang in there, honey, we'll get you. How far down do you think you are, about twelve feet?"

"At least." That meant she still had a long way to fall.

"Can you climb at all?" Murph asked.

"No, it's too slick."

She heard a blur of frightened voices, speaking words she couldn't understand. "What are you waiting for? Go get the rope!"

"We've got something that I think'll work," Murph called down. "Hold on for another moment."

She almost felt icy fingers of darkness groping for her.

"Sable," Murph called. "We have a rope of sorts. Reach up and I'll try to place it directly into your hands."

Balancing cautiously, she groped upward with her left hand and waited, terrified that the ledge would give way, or that the wind would whip her from her unsteady perch.

"Where is it?" she asked.

"It's not long enough," she heard Audry say. "How can we make it longer? Hurry, people, think, or she's going to fall!"

"Sable," Murph called down. "Can you try to climb just a little way?"

"No!" Sable shouted. "Not on this ice!"

"Just do it!" Murph ordered.

Her feet kept sliding, and she had to scramble for traction that wasn't there. She reached upward in desperation, scrabbling at ice-coated stubble and imbedded boulders. If not for Audry's penlight, the darkness would have been complete.

"Hold the line steady," Murph told the others. "I'm going to use it to climb down to her."

"No!" she cried. To her amazement, her fingers encountered a dry patch of earth over her head, where the ice must have broken loose. She dug into the soft mesh of roots and dirt, gained a handhold and pulled herself upward a few more inches.

Again she reached above her head, and her fingers touched something dangling. She stretched out and grasped the tip. It felt like leather. A belt?

"I've got it!" she shouted.

Murph called down to her, "Wrap it around your arm and let me pull you up."

"It isn't long enough. I can barely reach it." She tightened her grip, balanced on one foot, and kicked into a layer of ice to reach the dirt beneath. Miraculously, she gained a toehold and stepped up.

Just then the ledge beneath her other foot crumbled. She grasped the belt with both hands and kicked again at the hillside in one more desperate attempt to gain traction. To her relief, she found another soft spot.

She wrapped the leather around her arm and held on, praying that the lifeline wouldn't break, that Murph and the others wouldn't drop her.

"Pull me up!" Her arms began to quiver. She could find no

more toeholds. She could only hang on as she was being pulled, her shoulders protesting in pain as the rocky cliff gouged at her legs and arms. Every moment, she expected to lose her grip.

"Sable, you're getting close," Murph called from directly above her. "Reach up and I'll grab your hand."

With help from Audry's light, Sable could distinguish Murph's dark form as he reached down for her. She kicked against the slick trunk of a cedar and reached upward. Her foot slipped from the cedar, and she lost her grip. She felt herself slipping backward, and she cried out.

Murph caught her, and he pulled her over the edge and into his arms. For a long moment, she buried her face against his shoulder, unwilling to let go.

"Sable, what happened?" he asked.

She clung to him until her breathing eased and the horror lost some of its sharpness. "I'll tell you about it later. Right now, let's get to the house."

Murph followed Sable onto the sheltered front porch of the two-story house as the others joined them.

"Home," Sable murmured to him, still breathing heavily.

"I thought we'd never make it," Perry Chadwick muttered. "How anyone could live at the back of—"

"Mr. Chadwick," Audry cut in, "enough of your complaints. If Sable hadn't been kind enough to invite us to stay here, we would be in dire circumstances." The lady peered into the house through one of the diamond-paned windows, then turned to Sable. "Honey, is someone at home? Looks like there's a light in there."

Murph glanced through the same window. "There's a fire in the fireplace."

"Do you mind if we go on inside?" Perry said with a trace of sarcasm in his voice. "Then we can satisfy our curiosity."

Murph tested the door. It swung open into the cozy warmth of a large, paneled living room. He led the way inside, peering up the curved staircase, glancing down a hallway that led toward the back of the house. A light glowed at the end of that hall. There was a closed door to their left, and another door stood ajar directly beside the long rock hearth of the fireplace.

"This is more like it." Perry placed his suitcase against the wall carefully, then rushed toward the fire.

Exclaiming with relief, the others followed suit. Murph observed the interplay of people. The driver, Jerri, had fiery red hair and rosy cheeks to match. He couldn't stop thinking about her revelation on the bus—that she was a substitute.

Sable strolled toward the far right hallway. "Mom?" she called. "Hello? Who's here?"

Murph pulled off his coat and dropped it beside the others. He wanted access to his weapon. He followed Sable.

The swinging door to the right revealed a kitchen, where a light glowed over the sink. The kitchen was not occupied. Murph caught barely a glimpse of it before Sable pressed past him and stepped into what proved to be a family room across the hallway.

In a few minutes, Murph received an abbreviated tour of the huge house, following Sable as she switched on a light in every room, along the upstairs hallway, with a cursory glance up the attic steps. They didn't find anyone.

Sable's increasing concern was obvious.

"Is there anyplace else someone might be?" he asked.

"I haven't looked in the basement or the garage." She shivered. "It's cold up here."

"Why don't you join the others at the fireplace. You've been through a lot, and we can't afford to have you sick."

"I need to know who's here."

He grasped her arm before she reached the stairs. She looked at him.

He slid the soaked sleeve of her sweater up her arm and felt the icy chill of her hands, the goose bumps on her flesh. He felt a quiver run through her.

"Stop," he said. Before she could protest, he grabbed an afghan from the nearest bedroom and wrapped it around her shoulders. "You're going downstairs to the fireplace right now, and I'll complete the search."

To his surprise, she didn't protest.

SIX

Sable shivered beneath the folds of the afghan. Murph was checking the garage for automobiles, which she should have considered immediately.

Perry leaned toward Jerri at the hearth, and Sable heard him mumble an apology for the accident with the flashlight.

Jerri patted his broad, fleshy shoulder, then pointed down at his leather-soled, black dress shoes. "May I suggest that next time you travel, you wear lug-soled boots?"

Sable pulled the afghan more snugly around her. Could that push have been an accident? Someone else could have slid, then bumped against her. But somehow she would have expected anyone with integrity to say, "Excuse me for pushing you off the mountain. How can I make it up to you?"

Audry bent over Sable. "While we're waiting to discover the identity of our mystery host, why don't you put me to work gathering towels and blankets for—"

The basement door at the end of the hearth opened suddenly, and a tall, dark-haired man entered.

Sable recognized him immediately. "Craig!"

His heavy brows tipped upward in surprise at the small crowd huddled around the fireplace. "Sable? What on earth are you doing back? Who's your company?"

Sable rushed forward and gave her old friend a quick hug, suddenly overwhelmed by relief. She felt his surprise at such an affectionate welcome, especially since she'd just seen him at her grandfather's funeral only two days ago.

"What are you doing down from the mountain?" she asked.

He glanced at the rest of the group, and then at Murph, who was returning from the garage.

Sable took Craig's arm and turned to the others. "Meet our nearest neighbor, Craig Holt. We can probably thank him for the fire and the unlocked door." She noticed Murph's suddenly intent look. "He's a family friend," she explained, turning back to Craig. "I tried calling here last night, but no one answered. I couldn't reach either of my brothers or Mom."

"Weather got bad soon after you left yesterday, so your mom drove to Eureka Springs earlier than she'd planned to stay with Randy," Craig explained. "And the phone line's down. What are you doing back so soon?" He gestured toward the others. "It isn't the best of weather for a house party."

"They're passengers on our bus. We're stranded."

"Bus?" Craig said. "In this weather? Why would you take a bus when you—"

"I'll explain it all later," Sable assured him.

Craig shrugged. "Your mom wanted me to keep an eye on things while she was gone. With the ice storm, I thought I'd just stay for a couple of days. No use trying to get home from here, and I'm sure not going to try to drive in this mess.

"So that's your Jeep in the garage?" Murph asked.

Craig nodded, giving Murph a silent once-over.

Sable asked Craig to round up some towels, and he seemed eager to escape the small group of strangers.

The attic was filled with old clothes accumulated over the years. There were sure to be things that would fit the guests.

She thought about the safe, hidden deep behind the antiques, old furniture and storage boxes. She had never paid much attention to it, except when she and her brothers had played up there as children, imagining the heavy old safe to be stuffed with stolen cash or gold pieces or treasure maps.

At this point, she hoped it contained something more

precious—proof of Grandpa's innocence. If only she knew the combination.

While Simmons, Perry, Jerri, Audry and Bryce spread their wet coats over the bricks of the raised hearth, Sable glanced toward Murph. In the six weeks since he had come to work at the clinic, she had found him to be kind to patients, attentive to details and extremely attractive. His appeal was undeniable— from the dark-lashed green eyes and dark auburn hair to the broad shoulders. Patients and staff trusted him. He was willing to help his colleagues, without needing credit.

Sable also sensed that maybe he wasn't as open and uncomplicated as he initially appeared. Now, however, he represented solidity in a world of shifting foundations.

She pulled off her shoes and socks, rolled up the legs of her jeans, and sank her bare feet into the warmth of the deep carpet while she watched Murph with the others. When he turned toward her, she looked away.

Audry inspected an antique brass planter containing a thick silk fern, then stepped to the cabinet filled with antique figurines. "Some of these things must be older than I am. Probably in better working order, as well. Beautiful job of decorating."

"Thank you," Sable said.

"You did this? And the drapes, the paneling, those mirrors in the corner?"

"The paneling has been here as long as I can remember. My grandfather and mother and I redecorated the house together last summer. I supervised. Mom did the sewing, and Grandpa did the heavy lifting." She studied the small rocks in one of Grandpa's display cases, turned to Audry, then frowned and looked back at the rocks. There was something different about them….

Craig came back down the stairs with an armful of mismatched towels. "Come and get 'em," he said.

Audry reached for a small hand towel and gave it to Sable. "Honey, I think you need to step closer to the fire. Your hair is still wet." She took Sable's arm and gently urged her forward. "Where is your grandfather now?"

"We…had his funeral this week."

Audry lost her grip on Sable's arm. Her face paled noticeably in the dim flicker of the fire.

"Audry? Are you okay?"

For a moment, the woman didn't respond. She pressed her hands against her cheeks, closed her eyes and took a slow, deep breath. "Forgive me. I…suppose the excitement must have upset me more than I thought."

"Do you feel weak?" Sable asked. "Are you in pain?"

Audry opened her eyes. "I'll be fine. Don't worry about me." She sighed. "I'm so sorry to hear about your grandfather."

"Thank you. I'm sure you'll feel better with some warm clothing." She gestured to the others. "Craig, would you show everyone to the attic where there are extra clothes? I'm going to change quickly and make some warm drinks to knock off the chill."

Those who had brought overnight cases went upstairs to change, while Craig led the others to the attic. Sable changed quickly in her own room, then went to her mother's bedroom on the first floor.

The bed was unmade, and Sable caught sight of a faded, pea-green backpack tossed into the far corner of the room. It was Craig's—she'd seen it many times when he'd gone hiking with Randy and Peter. For a moment, she felt uncomfortable about anyone—even a family friend—moving into her mother's bedroom while she was away. It made sense, however, to stay downstairs, near the fire. After all, Craig had spent plenty of time here, hanging out with her brothers, listening to Grandpa's stories, exploring the cave.

Sable reached for the telephone atop Mom's bedside stand. The line was dead. Jerri might still be able to reach dispatch through Grandpa's broadband radio in the family room.

Sable opened the top drawer of her mother's nightstand, where Mom kept all her most recent correspondence. The drawer was a disorganized mess, totally expected for Mom, especially during a time of crisis. Grandpa's death had hit her hard.

Sympathy cards were mixed with grocery receipts and bills. Most of the unopened envelopes were probably sympathy cards, but the envelopes could contain anything.

Mom had never handled grief well, and she was prone to depression. When Dad died, Mom's meticulous world had collapsed for many months afterward, which was why she'd moved back here to be with her father. Sable and her brothers had learned many years ago not to talk to their mother about the death of a loved one.

This past week, Sable had attempted to explain to Mom the change of heart—the change of life—that she and Grandpa had experienced at Christmas, when Noah Erwin had explained to them the true power of Christmas. On Christmas night, less than two months ago, Sable and Grandpa had become committed followers of Christ, and Josiah Kessinger had lived the final few weeks of his life with newfound faith.

Mom had refused to listen. "If that gives you comfort, Sable, then you cling to that," she'd said gently. "I'll remember my father in my own way."

Grandpa's new faith did give Sable peace.

Sable found a recent letter with Grandpa's Freemont return address, which she slid into the front pocket of her slacks. She placed everything else back into the drawer and closed it.

The second drawer in her mother's bureau contained tax records that Sable had organized at Christmas. On top of it all was an unopened business envelope addressed in type to this house, with no return address.

Sable opened the envelope, pulled out one sheet of folded paper and read.

My Dear Family,

I'm not sure what words to use that will explain what I'm doing. I only hope that someday you will forgive and accept. It's been more than eleven years since Grandma died, and I've never looked back, never considered anything like this before.

By the time you get this letter, you will have heard the story. I'm sorry for the trouble this will cause you. I'm sorry I'll miss Sable's birthday party this year, because I know how she loves them. Sable, you'll have to accept the watch for a combination Christmas and birthday gift this time. Don't try to take on my guilt. I'm no longer afraid of the truth. Don't worry, I'm safe in the afterlife.

I now request forgiveness for the fraud connected with our purchase and attempted resale of the mine back on the old Seitz place. The buyer checked the mine thoroughly and discovered what others had overlooked. The walls were salted with sphalerite and galena from elsewhere. I must confess, and I leave my guilt in the hands of Christ.

But still, there is so much more involved here.

May God Help Me,

Josiah D. Kessinger

"Oh, Grandpa," she whispered. "You *did* it? You really *did?*" She sank onto Mom's bed, bewildered. Devastated.

Josiah Kessinger—who had always been there for her, whom she had admired and loved, who had shared his heart and home with her whole family—was confessing to fraud?

Grandpa...

This past week she'd comforted herself with the assurance that her grandfather wouldn't do what Otis Boswell and the police had accused him of doing. She'd been sure his name would be cleared because of the integrity with which he'd lived.

That foundation of comfort began to crumble.

She stuffed the note into the front pocket of her slacks. She couldn't think about it right now. She *couldn't* believe it!

She heard a squeak of floorboards just outside the room. She had pulled the latch that locked the ancient doors, of course, but the knob of the right door turned slowly.

She stiffened and held her breath.

SEVEN

"Who's there?" Sable called sharply.

The knob stopped rattling, and the floor creaked again. Sable rushed to the door and jerked it open to find Craig Holt backing away, his tall frame slouched, as usual, a huge silhouette outlined by the firelight.

"Sorry, Sable," he said, obviously embarrassed. "I thought you'd be changing in your own bedroom upstairs."

"I'm not changing, I'm looking through some papers."

"Guess it was a little slick getting here. You okay? You don't look the best."

"Thanks," she said drily. This was the Craig Holt she knew. At twenty-nine, he still retained many of the boyish qualities her brothers had outgrown. Still terminally shy around most women, he preferred hunting and fishing over any other social activity, and he was a die-hard spelunker. A few years ago, he had made a few awkward attempts to ask her on a date. She'd been too busy studying medicine to pay much attention.

"Where's your car?" he asked. "Why'd you take the bus?"

"The car's...I wrecked it."

"What! You wrecked that Camaro?" He made it sound like a personal affront. "When?"

"Last night."

"Oh, man, that stinks. How bad?"

Sable shook her head, comforted by the predictable response. "Thanks, I'm fine, but I appreciate the concern."

"Sorry, but you're obviously okay."

"The Camaro's gone. It went into the canal down by Freemont. I'll tell you all about it later. Right now, I think I'd better see to our guests."

"Oh, yeah, sure." Craig hesitated, already backing away. "Well, I think I'll bring in some more wood for the furnace."

She watched him walk away, shaking his head, and she knew he was grieving the loss of the Camaro.

When he opened the front door, Sable heard the hiss of rain slapping on the icy ground. It would be light soon. The darkness was already lifting, though in this hollow it would be hours before the sun would appear—if it came out at all today. The thermometer read twenty-nine degrees.

Simmons came down the stairs, his curly brown hair hanging in wet ringlets around his face. He wore an old, red plaid shirt that had once been Peter's favorite. Simmons's thick, muscular neck prevented him from closing the top button, but the shirt hung in folds around his midriff.

"Somebody get overheated?" he complained as he reached for the door to close it.

Just then, Craig came barreling through with an armload of wood. "Oh, good," he said when he saw Simmons standing there, "you look like you could carry a few sticks of wood without much trouble. Want to bring in another armload or two?"

Simmons joined him.

Sable went to the kitchen. Already, she missed the peace that had always greeted her when she came home. Tonight, home didn't offer the safety and seclusion she desperately needed. She felt vulnerable.

Had she and Murph been followed from Freemont, in spite of their precautions? Could her fall have been a deliberate attempt to hurt her?

The kitchen held Sable's sweetest memories; she and Grandpa had spent so many hours renovating it. From the smooth brick floor to the thick pine ceiling beams, she felt his presence. He'd carved the beams himself.

The pain of his loss filled her again. How she missed him, and how she ached from the words of his letter.

She leaned against the work island in the middle of the large kitchen, admiring, as always, the beautiful counters that Grandpa had inlaid. In the dining room, she could see the corner of the rustic table with split log benches, also handmade by Grandpa. Everywhere, the reminders both saddened and warmed her.

She picked up a kettle and carried it to the double sink. Waxing nostalgic, she grasped the bright red handle of the old water pump and worked it up and down. After a little exercise, she was rewarded by a healthy stream of water from the spout. She filled the kettle and carried it past the antique woodstove to the modern electric stove on the far wall. The pump and the woodstove came in handy during bad weather. The electricity in this old house wasn't reliable.

She lit a burner, left the water to heat and went upstairs. She needed to make sure the old safe was still securely locked.

The long, L-shaped upstairs hallway glowed with the light of electric lamps in three of the small alcoves. Colorful oil lamps stood on polished wooden shelves at intervals in the paneled hall—cleaned and ready in case of a power outage.

The house was well insulated, partially recessed into the hill behind it, which helped warm it in the winter and cool it in the summer. Sable had fond memories of the tricks she'd played on her brothers during childhood games of hide-and-seek. She'd climbed from the sewing room window on the second floor onto the cliff just inches from the window ledge. Then she'd scaled the rocky crag up one floor, scampered over to the attic window and climbed back inside.

After the third or fourth time, Peter had caught on and locked the windows, leaving her outside on the ledge.

In addition to the sewing room, the second floor had four bedrooms and two bathrooms. The floor below had two more bedrooms and another bathroom. Enough space for plenty of people to stay comfortably. Under ordinary circumstances.

She found Murph standing beside the dresser in her bedroom at the end of the hall, studying an old photograph album.

He looked up when she entered, holding up the book. "I recognize Otis Boswell and your grandfather." He pointed to one of the photos. "Who's this other man?"

She leaned close and saw the familiar, beloved face of Grandpa in his old camouflage hunting cap, grinning as he held his rifle balanced across his shoulder. To his right stood Otis Boswell, at least six inches shorter and twice as broad. The third man was taller than Grandpa, with black hair and a familiar, warm smile.

"That's Reuben Holt," she said. "Craig's father."

"Craig's father was also friends with Boswell?"

"I wouldn't call them friends, exactly. Grandpa and Boswell hunted on Reuben's property a few times, with Reuben's permission. Reuben and his wife, Camilla, moved to Jefferson City a few months ago. Reuben's running for the state senate."

"Craig is living in the middle of the Mark Twain National Forest by himself?" Murph asked. "A young man like him?"

She shrugged. "Craig's an outdoorsman, and he owns a marina near Eagle Rock."

"You know him pretty well?" Murph asked.

"Very. Craig was a good friend to both my brothers. He was always hanging around here."

"How well did he know your grandfather?"

"Very."

"And Boswell?"

"The Holts never seemed to care much for Otis Boswell. Why the questions, Murph? What are you thinking?"

"I wonder if the Holts might know something we don't."

"About Boswell?"

Murph closed the album. "If Josiah Kessinger didn't salt that mine, and Noah Erwin didn't salt it, it stands to reason their other partner did."

With a pang, Sable thought about the note in her pocket.

Grandpa had condemned himself with his own words. She needed to find out who had killed Noah. If Grandpa truly was guilty of fraud—and she still wasn't convinced that he was—she needed to know the extent of his culpability.

"I'll ask Craig what he knows," she said.

"Not tonight. I don't think we need to tell anyone about all this yet." Murph's expression softened. "Sorry, I don't want to worry you, I just opened the chest looking for blankets and found this photo album."

The pleasantly aromatic scent of cedar pervaded the room as Murph helped Sable pull out two stacks of quilts and blankets.

Sable closed the chest, her thoughts awash once again in memories. "Grandpa made this chest for me years ago. I wanted him to make it out of cedar, and he wanted to work with oak. We argued about it for three days, until he gave in. After all, as I put it, if it was a gift for me, I should have my choice."

"So you inherited your strong will from your grandfather."

"You might say that." She inhaled the fragrance of cedar again, and then she grew aware of Murph's sudden, watchful silence.

"What's on your mind?" she asked.

"Otis Boswell. The more I learn about the man, the less I like him." Murph glanced toward the door, then leaned closer. "That man is not your friend."

She grimaced. That appeared to be true. "Why not?"

"He personally came to the clinic and questioned us while you were away at the funeral this week."

"About what?"

"I don't know what he asked the others. He asked me if I'd seen you carrying any papers home with you after hours."

"Papers from the clinic?" she exclaimed. "That doesn't have anything to do with the Seitz mine."

"You're right, it doesn't."

She slid her hand into the front pocket of her slacks and

touched the corner of her grandfather's note. "There's something else going on there, Murph. I know there is."

"Is that the loving devoted granddaughter talking, or the logical mind of Dr. Sable Chamberlin?"

"Logic. Grandpa was a good man, not a defrauder. He especially would not defraud a friend like Noah."

"That's what Noah said."

"I'll do all I can to uncover the truth about Grandpa's involvement with the mine, and if I find proof that he did salt it, I'll see that the injured parties are compensated, even if I have to pay for it out of my own pocket. But there's no way the Josiah Kessinger I knew would ever have done what he's been accused of doing, and even less so since Christmas, when he became a Christian, thanks to Noah's influence."

There was a discernible softening of Murph's expression, a tenderness in his eyes. "Leave it to Noah." He turned away abruptly and stepped to the window.

She watched him. "Murph?"

He cleared his throat, took a slow, deep breath and released it. "Looks like it's up to us to find what we need to find here."

She wanted to show him the note, and she would. At the moment, though, the sting of it was too fresh.

Murph turned to look at her, and his attention focused on the watch Sable wore around her neck. "Beautiful craftsmanship. It no longer runs?"

"It has sentimental value. Grandpa carried it in his pocket for years."

"You loved him very much."

"He was the main man in my life after my father died."

Murph nodded slowly. "He did a great job."

"Thank you."

"Since the two of you were so close, did he ever mention anything to you about his concerns in Freemont?"

"Nothing." And now she was regretting that. "He was one of those tough guys who don't like the women and children to worry." *What else were you hiding, Grandpa?*

Murph nodded. "I know the type. It runs in my family, too. But that means we have to start from scratch."

"Yes, and we're on our own."

"Of course." Apparently, he caught some inflection in her voice, and he frowned at her.

"I didn't slip down that cliff tonight, I was pushed."

A pulse of adrenaline snapped through Murph like a bullwhip. "Pushed! Who—"

"I don't know. Ever since it happened, I've tried to convince myself I imagined it, but what if—"

"—someone followed us from Freemont?" He exhaled a long breath. "I wish you'd told me sooner."

"In front of the guests? I haven't had a chance to tell you privately."

"They aren't guests," Murph said. "We don't really know who they are." Right now he wanted to find out, fast.

"We can't afford to alert anyone that we suspect. I'm still hoping it was somehow a mistake."

"We can't take that chance."

"We can't panic the whole house on a suspicion. I—"

"Hello! Knock, knock." Audry's brisk voice rang out from the open doorway of the bedroom.

Murph looked around in surprise, and heard Sable's gasp.

"Audry," Sable said. "You startled me."

"Looks that way." Audry entered the room. "Sorry, honey, but we need these quickly. Everyone is still chilled." She reached for some of the blankets and carried them out, her footsteps echoing down the hallway.

"You were saying?" Murph prompted Sable.

She picked up some quilts. "I don't want to say anything about it to the others. Not yet. Would you carry these downstairs? I'm going to check the attic."

"Alone?"

"As long as the others are downstairs, I'm perfectly safe."

"People are wandering all over the house. We can't keep track of everyone."

"Just go. I'll be down in a moment."

Murph did as he was told. But he didn't like it.

EIGHT

Murph stood in the middle of the room with a pile of blankets under his arm, watching Perry the chubby man and Jerri the substitute bus driver circulate among the others with mugs of steaming coffee and cocoa.

When he saw Sable coming down the stairs, he raised an eyebrow in a silent inquiry. She gave a reassuring nod. The safe was apparently secure in the attic.

"Special brew for our hostess." Perry's fleshy cheeks stretched in a grin. He handed Sable a mug of hot chocolate as she took the final step into the living room. "You probably saved our lives and nearly lost yours, so you get the last cinnamon stick."

Audry took a quilt from Murph. "No need for you to take care of the rest of us, Murph. We all might as well make ourselves useful." She shot an impatient look at Simmons, who was sprawled across the sofa, brooding in front of the fire.

Murph ambled across the room, studying first young Bryce, then Simmons. He turned again to Sable, who peered at the others through the steam rising from her mug. Her expression reflected his own uneasiness.

"Do you have a farm, Sable?" Bryce gestured toward a picture on the wall of the black Angus bull posed with two young guys, apparently Sable's brothers.

"Not anymore. My grandfather sold all the farm animals."

"All but the dog," Craig said. "I've been taking care of him."

Sable's neighbor glanced out the window at the gray, storming sky, then sat on the hearth beside the stack of logs. "Sable's got an honest-to-goodness cave here, with ghosts."

Murph suppressed a smile at Craig's youthful exuberance. He seemed much younger than he looked.

"Ghosts." Bryce's tone left no doubt about his disdain.

"Ask Sable," Craig said. "Her family lived with the legend."

Bryce looked at Sable, scorn still in place.

She took another sip of her chocolate and sat next to Craig on the hearth. "He's talking about a story that accompanied the cave when my grandfather took over this place thirty years ago," she said. "Two brothers from New York bought the property in the early forties, intending to mine it for zinc and lead. Unfortunately for them, the man who'd sold it claimed it had rich deposits of ore."

"They bought it without checking it out?" Bryce asked.

"No," Sable said, "they checked it and found galena and sphalerite, the ores for lead and zinc, but later they discovered they'd been tricked. Someone had planted the ores in the cave. That's what is called 'salting a mine.'"

"How is that done?" Bryce asked.

Sable hesitated, closed her eyes for a very brief moment as an expression of darkness crossed her face. "It was probably shot into the walls with a gun to make it look as if the ore was imbedded."

"But when the men explored further," Craig said, picking up the story, "word spread that they'd discovered silver."

"Silver!" Bryce exclaimed.

"Craig, don't lead him on like that," Sable warned. "It was just a rumor."

Craig ignored her. "Somebody offered the partners an outrageous amount of money for the cave."

"Every tale about this cave is different," Sable said. "Both partners disappeared. This part of the country had a flood about that time, and the community was preoccupied with the rising rivers, so nobody searched for the owners."

While Sable told the story, Murph surreptitiously studied each face in turn. Craig sat watching Sable with rapt attention, like a love-struck schoolboy…or maybe that was Murph's imagination.

"Later, neighbors did search for the men," Sable continued. "They even wrote to New York. No reply."

Murph looked at Simmons, who hadn't moved from his position on the sofa. Audry wandered around the room, looking at family pictures, studying figurines. Perry Chadwick had returned to the kitchen, possibly to rustle up some food. He didn't appear to have missed many meals.

"The land passed down the family line," Sable continued, "and then a nephew of those two men sold it to my grandfather."

"Legend has it that the ghosts of the two men guard the treasure." Craig made his voice dramatically spooky.

"What legend?" Sable razzed him. "There's no legend."

Craig ignored her. "Sable's grandpa figured out the ghost activity. The barometer rises and falls in a cave the way it does outside, creating a draft. That causes the door at the cave's entrance to open and close all by itself."

Bryce's shoulders slumped. "That's all there is to it?"

"Sorry to be such a disappointment to you," Sable said dryly. "Nothing's ever haunted us here."

"Can I explore the cave?" Bryce asked.

"If we're stuck here long enough," she said.

"All right!"

"And if you want to study a map first," Craig said, "there's one up on the wall in the attic. Josiah did all the surveying and drew it up himself. It's pretty close to scale."

Jerri strolled into the room, her muscular arms crossed over her chest and her red hair spiked as if she'd been combing it with her fingers. "I just reported in. Thanks for the use of your radio, Sable. I got to it just in time, the batteries are almost dead. We've got to stay put for the time being."

Perry yawned and stretched like a plump cat. "I think I'll prepare for bed, if nobody minds."

The others agreed that they were ready to retire, too, and

Sable assigned rooms, giving the second downstairs bedroom to Bryce. The rest were upstairs.

"If it's okay with you, Sable," Perry said, "I'll use the cot in the sewing room upstairs. I've been told I snore like a semi truck. It's the weight, you know."

Murph agreed to share a room with Simmons, though he hated the thought of sleeping with the pistol gouging his ribs. To his dismay, he learned from Sable that the room had bunk beds. His six-foot-one-inch frame would not fit easily into a bunk.

As everyone retired, and Murph entered the room he was to share, a duffel bag sailed past his left elbow and landed on the lower bunk.

"First dibs," Simmons called behind him. He flopped onto the mattress, shoes and all. "I hate heights. Mind turning off the light?"

The sound of footsteps and muffled voices upstairs diminished as Sable settled in front of the living room fireplace. She allowed herself the luxury of distant memories.

She remembered sitting flanked by her brothers, staring into the flames while Grandpa perched on the stone hearth across from them, his blue eyes sparkling as he wove an exciting, spur-of-the-moment tale.

The stories he'd told the three of them were always fiction. At least, the ones he'd called *stories* were, but when Sable was alone with him, they'd shared dreams. Grandpa's dream had always been to send his grandchildren to college.

He'd paid to see those dreams come true. Only later did Sable discover that the tuition money had come as a loan from his business partner, Otis Boswell.

Sable pulled out the letter she had stuffed into her pocket along with the confession note. Setting the note aside, she scanned the first two pages of the last letter Grandpa had written to Mom, dated December 20.

The last page caught her attention. *I have a surprise for you and the kids,* it read. Grandpa always had a surprise of some kind.

Not sure about it yet, but I know it's there. Don't want to ruin it.
The remainder of the letter, written in his usual flamboyant style,
said nothing more about it.

What could he have been talking about? Maybe the Seitz
mine? He'd been so sure it would sell and he would be out of
debt for good. But that was no secret.

A quiet movement startled her. She turned to find Murph
standing on the stairs. His auburn hair had dried, and he wore
jeans that were too short for him. An old, faded blue turtleneck
of Peter's peeped out from beneath a baggy, ragged denim
hunting shirt of Grandpa's.

"Nice fashion statement," she teased. "That shirt must be at
least twenty years old."

"I'm a paramedic, not a model." He chuckled and shoved the
sleeves of the shirt up to his elbows as he padded barefoot down
the stairs and across the carpet to join her.

He sat next to her and rested an arm across the back of the
sofa. "How are you holding up?"

"Part of me is so tired I want to crawl into my bed and sleep
for a week. Another part feels I may never sleep again."

"It was rough up on that cliff," he said quietly. "For a moment,
I was afraid we'd lost you."

"So was I. You're pretty good in an emergency."

"It was Bryce who suggested fastening our belts together for
a rope. Good thing Perry Chadwick has a big waist."

"I barely reached it as it was," she said.

He gently touched a tender spot on her chin. "It's turning a
pretty shade of purple. Did it happen when you fell?"

"It must have."

"Are there medical supplies here in the house? The way things
are going, we'll need them."

"I have a supply in my bedroom." She examined the scratches
on his neck. "You could use something on those."

"Yes, Doctor." He reached down and touched a series of
scratches on the back of her hand. "Physician, heal thyself." His
voice sounded…almost intimate.

Sable wanted to bask in his reassuring strength, but she knew that was a response to the fear that stalked her.

They sat in weary silence for several moments, then Murph gestured to the letter she had placed on the arm of the sofa. "Is that from Josiah? Looks like his handwriting."

"How would you recognize Grandpa's handwriting?"

He picked up the pages. "I've seen his signature. He wrote with such flair."

He fell silent as he deciphered the script, then he sat back. "Did he give any hint about the surprise mentioned here?"

"Not that I recall."

Murph handed the letter back to Sable. "We should look for hard evidence that could incriminate someone for the Seitz mine debacle, for Noah's death and for Josiah's death."

"Josiah's?" she exclaimed. "You think someone killed my grandfather?"

"You told me Josiah collected incriminating evidence against someone. Why would the perpetrator allow him to live?"

Sable gave that thought time to register. It shocked her. It infuriated her. And then she thought once more about the confession letter. Why would he write that? It made no sense.

"We have to examine anything we find without preconceived notions," Murph said.

"If we can find anything to examine." Sable stood up and walked to the fire. "The day after my grandfather's death, Otis Boswell paid me a call with two of Freemont's finest."

"The police?"

Sable nodded. "He grilled me about Grandpa and flat out told me that my grandfather was a criminal. Then he tried to make it look as if I was an accomplice."

There was a long silence, and Sable turned to find Murph's eyes blazing.

"I didn't tell anyone about it," she said. "Not even Noah, who was our closest friend in Freemont."

Murph stood up and stepped to her side. He placed an arm around her shoulders. "Boswell again," he said. "You've got to realize that man's as dirty as they come. It had to be hard for you to hear that about your grandfather."

"It was devastating."

"We've both been devastated this week."

She sat down on the raised stonework of the hearth. Something in Murph's tone registered. She'd heard the sound of grief in his voice earlier. She remembered his shock when she'd told him of Noah's death. More than shock. It had been more like stunned grief.

"How long did you know him?" she asked softly.

Murph didn't reply.

"What haven't you told me?" she asked.

He closed his eyes. With a deep sigh, he rubbed his face with his hands, then looked at her again. "Noah was my uncle."

NINE

Sable stared at the man she thought she'd come to know well in the past six weeks. Murph, who had a big heart, a deft hand with patients and a good attitude with the rest of the staff, suddenly seemed like a stranger.

"Your uncle! Why the secrecy?"

He joined her on the raised hearth. "Noah called me a few months ago about some concerns he had. He wanted me to investigate Boswell Mining. He'd invested his life's savings into that Seitz property. He and Josiah were both worried when Josiah found a different title to that property."

Sable could only stare at Murph. "He never told me."

"According to the old title," Murph said, "there were previously productive galena mines in a circumference around the Seitz land."

So *that* was what Grandpa had been talking about when he suggested that he was concerned about some discrepancies. She was no miner, but she'd learned enough about mines to know that if there had been ore all around the property, that center part would have been barren. It was a well-known fact among miners.

"So the land had been misrepresented to them in the first place," she said.

"Exactly," Murph said. "Then Boswell gave an agent orders to sell. The agent misrepresented it, against the wishes of Noah and Josiah, and the new prospector became suspicious and checked it out."

"But Grandpa took the blame in spite of his protests."

"Noah told me about some events in Freemont recently," Murph said. "The mining accidents, shoddy safety standards...a couple of people have disappeared."

Sable reached into her pocket, grasped the corner of Grandpa's letter, and pulled it out with a sigh. "In light of what you're saying, this might throw a kink in the works."

She handed it to Murph. "I found it in an unopened envelope in my mother's bedside stand," she said.

They read it together. As Sable studied the words for the second time, she noticed something she'd missed before: the mention of missing her birthday party. She hated birthday parties. So why would her grandfather write that?

She knew it was his writing; his flamboyant style was not easily forged. She just couldn't bear the words, that, indeed, sounded like a confession.

Grandpa, how could you?

"This doesn't fit," Murph said when he'd finished reading. "Why would he confess to fraud when he was collecting evidence about someone else's criminal activities?"

"I wish I knew."

"What an awful blow this has been," Murph said. "This letter mentions your birthday. When is it?"

"The day after Valentine's Day."

"This coming Tuesday. How old? Or is it impolite to ask?"

She appreciated the obvious diversion. "Thirty-one." She rubbed her eyes, reconsidered the words she'd read and looked at the letter again. "Tell me if you think there's something about this that doesn't ring true."

He leaned over her shoulder to look at it.

"It isn't Grandpa's style," she said. "This letter rambles about things that don't make sense. All his other letters have been logical and direct."

"I agree."

She studied the note a moment longer, then folded it and put it back in her pocket. "Maybe I'm just trying too hard to excuse away these words."

"Your grandfather influenced your life in many ways," Murph said. "You've got to remember that the Josiah Kessinger who died in that wreck was a new man. If this note is true—and I'm not convinced it is—then maybe the guilt he felt about what he'd done was what drew him to Christ in the first place."

"And so I'm supposed to be happy about it?" She regretted the bitterness that crept into her voice.

"No, but you should withhold judgment until you know the truth."

Murph's words, spoken with quiet sincerity, didn't ease her pain. "I never thought there would be shame in being Josiah Kessinger's granddaughter."

"Never be ashamed of who you are. You might have inherited your Grandpa's impulsive nature, too." He tapped her gently on the arm. "Along with his strength of will."

"I wonder who gave the order to those goons who chased us last night," Sable said.

"So do I."

They stared into the flames as if a message might come to them in the spiral of smoke that drifted lazily upward.

Something thumped against the front storm door. Sable froze. Murph leaped to his feet and pivoted, placing himself between Sable and the door.

The thump came again, then a familiar scratching on the screen. Sable went weak with relief, reminding herself to breathe. They were certainly on edge.

"It's Dillon." She stepped around Murph and walked to the front door.

The furry head of a drenched German shepherd shoved through the doorway as soon as Sable unlatched the door. He barked, jumping up to splash her around the waist with his soggy paws. His tongue flicked out and caught her across the mouth before she could pull away. She laughed, hugging him in spite

of the water and the smell of wet dog. He thumped his tail against
the paneled wall.

"That's enough, Dillon," she said, pushing him down. "Remember your manners."

Murph stepped forward. Dillon saw him and his lips drew
back in a challenging display of sharp, white fangs. His wet
hackles sprang up as a low growl rumbled from his throat.

"No, Dillon," Sable ordered. "It's okay. He's a friend." She
rested her hand on his head. "Friend."

Dillon relaxed. His fangs disappeared, and he looked up at her
with trusting eyes.

She glanced back at Murph. "Sorry. He's very protective."

"Will he bite if I pet him?"

"Not now. He understands the word *friend*." She reached for
a clean towel from the stack, unfolded it, knelt in front of the dog.
"Feet, Dillon. You know the routine."

Dillon sat and raised his left front foot, then his right one, for
Sable to pat dry. Then he stood at quiet attention and allowed her
to work on his back feet and coat. By the time she was finished,
the towel was soaking wet and Murph had made friends with
Dillon.

At Sable's command, the dog lay in front of the fire with his
head on his paws, his honey-brown gaze occasionally flicking
toward Sable as she and Murph returned to the sofa.

"He's beautiful," Murph said. "Does he understand *everything* you say?"

"Sometimes it seems like he does. Grandpa got him for all of
us, but Dillon and I have a special friendship. He can sense my
moods. Sometimes he's an embarrassing barometer of the way
I feel about guests in the house."

"You have a way with animals," Murph said.

"I like them. I guess they can tell."

He leaned forward and stroked Dillon's fur, then turned and
looked at Sable over his shoulder with a grin. "You have a way
with me," he said softly. "Does that mean you like me?"

"Of course, I like you," she said. "You're good with patients and helpful in ice storms."

He chuckled and sat back. For a few moments, they were content to listen to the crackle of the fire and the hiss and slap of the rain outside.

"What are your plans after you get out of this...mess?" Sable asked.

For a few seconds, he didn't answer, just stared into the fire. "I liked working in the clinic," he said. "But I also like the adrenaline rush of the emergency department. I'd planned to return to med school next year. I'm thinking I'd like to be an E.R. doc."

"You were in medical school? What happened?"

"My father had pancreatic cancer. My mother was taking care of him fine until they had a wreck on their way home from a chemo treatment one day. Mom had some broken ribs, and Dad was pretty bruised up."

"They needed you. And you came. And now?" she asked. "Don't they need you?"

"Dad went home just before Christmas." He looked at Sable. "His true home."

"I'm sorry for your loss," she said. "And now Noah."

"My losses aren't permanent." He nodded to Sable. "How about you? What do you plan to do?"

"I want to do just what Grandpa and I talked about when we sat this way years ago," Sable said. "I still want to be a country doc who knows all the patients she passes on the street, knows their kids' names, their parents' names and rubs shoulders with half her patients at the high school games."

Murph turned to look at her, and the firelight gave a smoky glow to the strong outline of his face, bathing his hair with reddish-gold highlights. His thick, dark brows showed a serious side that counterbalanced the great sense of humor she had seen, working with him at the clinic.

"Now that I know you're Noah's nephew," she said, "I don't understand how I missed the family resemblance. It's in the eyes...and in your heart."

* * *

In the light of the flickering fire and the gathering dawn, Murph watched Sable's eyelids droop.

"You'd better go upstairs before you collapse," he said.

She straightened her slender shoulders. "You too."

"And if we've been followed?"

"Dillon will sleep outside my room. He always does."

"Are you afraid someone will try to check out the attic while we're asleep?" Murph asked.

"Not with Dillon standing guard."

"I could post *myself* outside your room, at the door."

"Dillon will be more comfortable on the floor than you would," she said.

Dillon raised his head and yawned, then stretched, licked Murph's hand and blinked his eyes.

Sable stood and stretched, too, trying unsuccessfully to stifle a yawn. "You need sleep, Murph." Firelight danced against the heavy oak paneling of the room as Sable turned toward the fire.

Murph couldn't stop looking at her. She had delicate features, finely arched black brows and thick lashes. Her face was soft and feminine, with high cheekbones and a firm, defiant chin. She looked fragile, but appearances were misleading. He'd seen the steel in her character. This morning she was pensive, quieter than usual. That didn't stop his growing attraction to her, even under the circumstances—or perhaps *because* of the circumstances.

Without thinking, he stood and moved to touch her, then hesitated and dropped his hand. *What am I doing?*

Sable turned and smiled at him. Her smile faltered and she glanced toward the stairs. "You *are* going to nap?"

He nodded. "Be careful. Lock your door."

"I will." He saw that fear still lurked in her eyes. She turned away. "Good night."

Murph watched her go, bare feet silent on the carpeted steps. The black ringlets of her hair formed a halo around her shoulders from the soft lighting in the second floor hallway. Maybe it was the storm, or the excitement of the past week, but something about her affected him with increasing impact.

After she disappeared from view, his last image of her lingered. If only he could help ease the fear that haunted her eyes. If only he could be sure he was capable of protecting her. He wasn't even sure he could protect himself.

He stepped over to the fire to throw on another log. Dillon still dozed, and Murph touched the soft, fire-warmed fur on the dog's neck. He closed the tempered glass doors of the fireplace, then stepped outside to check the weather. The wind and rain met him like a glacier wall. In the gray distance, he heard icy limbs crashing to the ground.

He returned inside and closed the door. The ice glaze must be at least an inch thick by now.

The lamp by the window flickered and went out as he crossed the living room. The electric lines must be down. That wouldn't be a problem. He'd seen plenty of oil lamps upstairs, a hefty supply of batteries on the basement landing, and a wood furnace in the basement. Later today they would see about chopping more wood.

"Come on, Dillon," he called softly. "Upstairs. You need to keep watch over Sable."

The dog stretched to his feet from his comfortable perch by the fire and followed Murph up the stairs in the meager light of the stormy morning.

After seeing Dillon to Sable's door, Murph stepped into the bedroom he was sharing with Simmons. The moment he stepped through the door, he saw Simmons bolt upright in the gloom.

"Who is it?" he snapped.

"Your roomie. Paul Murphy." Murph wished he could get out of the clothes he was wearing and get comfortable, but that didn't look like a possibility for the near future. He noticed that Simmons braced himself up on one elbow, watchful, alert.

"You headed somewhere in particular?" Murph asked.

"No, I just hopped on the bus for a joyride," Simmons snapped. "What do you think?"

"So where are you headed?" Murph kept his voice conversational, blaming the man's irritability on fatigue.

"Home to Fayetteville," Simmons said at last. "My mother's dying in the hospital there, and my sisters called me yesterday to tell me to hurry." Simmons still sounded resentful, almost belligerent, and Murph wondered if he was telling the truth.

"I'm sorry to hear that," Murph said. "Maybe this ice will clear up and we can get you on your way before long."

"And you?" Simmons asked. "You and Sable are friendly enough. Could be you were hoping for a lot less company."

Murph didn't reply as he climbed onto the top bunk and lay on his side facing the room. He allowed himself to relax into the pillow, and reached upward for his real source of strength. *Lord, you brought me here for a reason. Now please guide me, guide Sable and heal our hearts. Help us depend on you alone...*

He was still hesitant to sleep, but even this dinky bunk bed felt seductively comfortable. He could hear Simmons's breathing, hypnotic and deep, its rhythm like a metronome, blending with the whisper of the rain outside....

TEN

A low rumble of thunder burst from the darkness and reverberated through Murph's chest, jolting him awake. His legs cramped, and he remembered he was in an upper bunk with a Detonics Pocket 9 pistol strapped to his chest so tightly it felt as if it had embedded into his flesh.

He'd fallen asleep in a room with a man he didn't trust. The pain reassured him that the gun remained in place. He reached up, feeling the cotton fabric of the shirt he'd rummaged from a box of old clothing in the attic last night. Good. He was covered.

The rumble came again. It wasn't Simmons snoring—no sound came from the lower bunk. It couldn't be thunder, because outside the window an invisible sun had turned the shrouded sky from pale gray to brilliant blue. The storm had passed.

The rumble became recognizable as the familiar sound of a dog's growl. Murph tossed back the warm blankets and climbed down from the top bunk. Simmons was already gone.

Shivering, Murph opened the door to find the German shepherd standing guard three doors down along the unlit hallway. Sable's room. The dog whirled around with a snarl when Murph stepped out.

"Quiet, boy."

Dillon's pointed ears relaxed.

"What is it? Do you need to go outside?"

Dillon whined and wagged his tail, then trotted over and thrust his wet nose into the palm of Murph's right hand.

"Okay, but let me get my shoes and socks on. I don't have as much fur on my feet as you do." With Dillon shadowing his steps, Murph returned to the bedroom to see if his socks had dried overnight. They hadn't. He'd have to dry them.

With shoes and socks in hand, he stepped over to the uncurtained window and looked out. The winter scene stunned him. Eighteen-inch icicles clung to the eaves of the house like sharpened spears. The dim shapes of crystal trees and rock cliffs hovered over the valley, like a picture on an Ozark postcard, all hills and valleys at sharp angles. Every inch was coated in ice.

Dillon growled again.

"I'm coming." He trailed downstairs after the dog, who waited patiently for Murph to spread his socks on the hearth.

Only a few live coals glowed amid the ashes. The temperature in the house must have dropped overnight into the low sixties, maybe lower. Murph restocked the fireplace with wood from a rack beside the hearth.

Meanwhile, Dillon sniffed at the basement door at the end of the wide hearth. He pawed at the door, then looked at Murph.

Reminded of an old Lassie show, Murph opened the door.

The dog leaped down the narrow steps, and with a growl disappeared into the darkness. Murph grabbed a flashlight from the shelf at the head of the stairway and joined the dog, who hovered at a short, open doorway about three feet square at the far end of the large concrete basement. Past the doorway was the gaping mouth of the cave.

Murph's love of caves had always attracted him to Missouri, which boasted more caves than any other state. More important right now, this cave seemed to be a source of fascination for Dillon.

Murph looked down at his bare feet, then back toward the entrance. His feet were tough.

He dropped to his knees and crawled through the cave mouth, shining his light ahead. A sound of shuffling reached him from the darkness, but before he could identify the source, Dillon barked.

Murph turned. The dog still hovered at the cave mouth, hackles raised. The sound didn't come again. Bats, maybe? Was there another entrance to this cave? Sable had said the cave would provide an escape if necessary.

A few feet farther, he discovered that the narrow mouth opened into a wide cavern. He straightened, inhaling the moist air while playing his light over gray-and-white formations. He studied the path, scoured by footprints in the solid, limestone floor. The path wandered past a regal column of white to a ledge of stone about twenty feet ahead. This natural wall blocked his view and cast the cavern into patches of shadow that undulated with the movement of the beam.

The sound came again from behind the rock ledge, a shuffling noise…like the cautious tread of a human foot.

"Hello?" Murph's hand tightened on the flashlight.

No answer.

"Sable? It's me. Murph. Are you back there?"

Silence.

He reached beneath his shirt and slid the holster into position, then crept forward, ducking beneath a stalactite. The shadows fell away as he stepped past the rock ledge, and the cavern opened into another room.

Someone darted out from the shadows of the ledge and stumbled against a boulder. Dillon barked.

The sudden glare of a flashlight split the darkness. The broad-shouldered figure straightened. Simmons.

"Out for a morning stroll?" Murph asked.

Simmons trained his light on the dog, who had joined Murph in the cave. "You got a problem with that?"

"Did you ask permission to come down here?"

There was an annoyed silence. "Did *you?*"

"Not unless you count Dillon's invitation." Murph leaned against a boulder and aimed his light around the walls of the cave. "Interesting place, isn't it?"

"Weird place," Simmons muttered. Murph noted the muscles that bulged beneath the long-sleeved T-shirt Simmons had found in the attic last night. He was probably about five-ten, which was three inches shorter than Murph. Murph guessed he weighed about 190, without an ounce of fat.

"I love caves," Murph said, aiming his light at some soda straw formations to the far right of the room. "It amazes me what God can do even in the absence of light."

Simmons gave a sudden snort. "You like to hang out with bats and talk about God?"

"If you don't like bats, what are *you* doing down here?"

Simmons brushed his fingers through his curly brown hair, which had frizzed from the moisture in the cave. "Think any of the passages lead anywhere? You know, like to civilization?"

"No one mentioned it last night, but it wouldn't hurt to ask. You must be in a hurry to get to the hospital."

Simmons aimed his flashlight up the side of the cave wall.

"I hope your mother's doing okay." Murph battled another frisson of discomfort, perhaps because of the way Simmons avoided meeting his gaze straight on. "I'm sorry you're stuck here, when you need to get out so badly."

Simmons lowered his flashlight, giving a long, deep sigh. "I wish I'd driven instead of taking that bus."

"Maybe we'll have a quick thaw, and you can be on your way." Nothing would make Murph happier.

"Guess we could go prospecting while we wait."

"Prospecting?"

"You know, for silver. Think there's anything to that story?"

"I doubt it. Missouri isn't known for silver mines. You know how easily stories get started."

"Wouldn't hurt to look, though, would it?"

Murph shrugged. "With permission from the owners."

Simmons raked the sides of the cave with his light once more. "Like I said, this place is weird." He stepped over some scattered rocks and onto the path, then left.

Dillon whined, looked up at Murph, then lowered his head, perked his ears and followed Simmons from the cave.

Murph nodded. "Good boy. Go to Sable. I'll be out in a

moment." But first, he wanted to check out a pit he had seen in the beam of Simmons's light. He stepped cautiously along the rock-strewn limestone. The pit seemed to swallow light, except for the jagged boulders around the rim, like teeth in the mouth of a giant serpent.

The mouth was big enough to swallow a small car. Murph's light barely touched the rocky bottom, about thirty-five feet below. Instinctively, he took a step backward. Anyone who fell down there could be badly injured—even killed.

"Better be careful over there," came a man's voice from behind him.

He spun around and saw Craig Holt in the cave entrance.

Murph picked his way carefully back toward the path. "That's quite a drop."

Craig shoved his hands into the pockets of his jeans and strolled forward. "If there's a drought, it's dry, if it's rainy or we have a lot of snowmelt, it's filled with water."

"You grew up with the Chamberlins?" Murph asked.

Craig nodded. "My sister and I used to come over all the time when we were younger. Sable and her brothers visited a lot, even before they moved in with Josiah. Whenever they were here, they'd call my sister and me, and we'd come over and help them get into mischief."

"You weren't afraid of the ghost?"

Craig laughed. It had a tight sound, as if he wasn't as relaxed as he wanted Murph to think. "Even as kids, we knew that rumors spread easily across these Ozark hills."

Murph peered back along the passage into the inky darkness. "Is the cave large?"

"We thought it was. We could spend a whole day down here and not cover it all." He glanced down at Murph's bare feet, and his black brows drew together. "Plan to do some exploring?"

"Not at the moment, but later, maybe. Spelunking is a favorite hobby of mine."

Craig turned and strolled ahead of Murph toward the house. "It's one of Sable's, too."

Murph thought he detected just a hint of possessiveness in the man's voice. He grimaced as Craig knelt to crawl out of the cave. This forced confinement was proving to be less and less comfortable.

ELEVEN

Sable was falling, her feet sliding down an icy ledge, and she couldn't stop the descent. She screamed into the darkness, and her eyes flew open to a sunny stream of light coming in through the window sheers.

She gripped the comforter to her chest and waited while her heart slowed. She didn't often have nightmares, and this one had been more a memory than a dream.

In spite of the cold air, perspiration dripped from her face and neck in tiny rivulets. She looked across the room at the pile of discarded clothes she had worn last night. From the front pocket of her crumpled slacks, a corner of the folded letters peeped out at her.

What was the surprise Grandpa had hinted about? Why did he have to be so obscure?

Tossing back the covers in frustration, she looked out the window beside her bed, where a bright sky was punctured by the bare, frozen branches of the old maple tree that grew beside the house. To her dismay, a bank of dark clouds formed a foreboding wall on the western horizon, creeping closer. She glanced at her watch. It was nearly noon. From experience, she knew that the sun would melt the ice just enough to make travel impossible today.

Her bumps and bruises protested when she climbed from bed, reminding her all too well of the past eighteen hours.

"Oh, Lord, protect me," she whispered into the silence of the room on her way to the window. "Protect all of us here."

She was new to the habit of prayer, but she had a feeling that she was about to get accustomed to it in the days to come—she'd never felt so helpless and lost in her life.

As she stepped between the gauzy blue curtains at the window, she gasped in wonder at the frozen, ice-white landscape below. Sparkling crystals coated even the slenderest of branches, making the trees look like the glass figurines she had admired in the gift shops in Branson.

Even the strongest oaks hadn't escaped damage from the weight of ice. Branches of all sizes littered the forest floor— falling branches were another danger for anyone who ventured outside.

As she marveled over the side-by-side beauty and destruction, a board creaked in the hallway. She stiffened and turned from the window. Hearing another creak, she recognized it. The sound came from the attic steps. This old house and its squeaky floorboards and settling timber…over the years she had learned the distinctive sound of each one.

She pulled on a terry robe and rushed to the door. When she turned the knob, the mechanism clicked. By the time she stepped out into the hallway, all she saw was a slender, gray-haired, female form disappear around the corner. Audry.

Something soft and fuzzy brushed against her leg, and she bit back a cry. A cold nose pressed against her hand. Dillon.

She knelt and hugged him, accepting a kiss from his wet tongue. "So you and Audry are friends, huh? I hope you didn't allow anybody else past this door. Go on downstairs. I'm up and on the alert again."

After dressing in old, faded jeans and a warm, sky-blue turtleneck that fit a little too snugly after eight years, Sable drew the blankets and the pink rosebud comforter over her pillows. She'd slept in her comfortable, private room on her solid bed while Murph and Simmons had squeezed into bunks. Perry had taken the rickety, uncomfortable cot in the sewing room.

She surveyed the room she had decorated last summer. The pale blue walls and silver-gray Berber carpeting were a perfect complement to the carved bureau, the antique lantern and washstand. She would probably be using the washstand. With no electricity, the only source of water was the hand pump in the kitchen. Someone would be kept busy carrying water upstairs.

Downstairs, a fire glowed in the hearth and the sound of footsteps reached her from the basement stairs. She hated the fear that made her heart beat faster and her muscles tense. But Dillon didn't bark. He didn't even react to the sound. Craig Holt entered, his thick, black hair tousled, soot on his chin, apparently from stoking the wood furnace.

Craig grinned at her. "What's the matter, sleepyhead? You look like you should've stayed in bed a couple more hours."

"And good morning to *you*," she said with the sarcasm that had always characterized their banter.

"Who's fixing breakfast? I'm starved."

Sable shook her head sadly. "Almost thirty and still looking for someone to fix your breakfast."

"Have your cooking skills improved?" Craig teased.

"Not much. Is there any food left in the freezer from the funeral dinner?"

"Some. Your mom took a couple of casseroles with her to Randy's, and she sent the fried chicken home with Peter. She gave me the roast."

"It's at your house, I guess," she said.

He shrugged. "I hadn't planned to move in down here."

"Great. What are we going to feed everybody?"

"Plenty in the pantry, and there's a lot of unprepared food in the freezer. As long as we don't open and close the door too much, it shouldn't thaw too fast." He glanced up the stairs. "Anybody else up? I saw Murph and Simmons earlier—they seemed to have an interest in the cave. And I thought I heard someone bumping around in the attic earlier this morning."

That must have been Audry.

Craig gave Dillon a quick scratch on the ears as he passed. "I fired up the wood furnace in the basement. Fortunately, there are plenty of limbs down outside. I'm going to draft some help chopping after breakfast."

"Good. I'll enlist someone to cook breakfast."

"Not you, I hope," he called over his shoulder as he stepped into the room he occupied. He closed the door before Sable could think of a proper retort.

Paul Murphy came from the basement, wiped his bare feet on the mat and gave her a nod. She couldn't help staring.

"Size twelve," he said, grinning at her. "Good morning."

"Craig reminded me it's almost noon. I think he's expecting someone to fix breakfast."

"Can't he cook?"

"Not if I can stop him before he does any damage."

Murph gestured toward the pair of socks on the hearth next to his shoes. "Sorry about the laundry in the middle of the living room."

"Does it take two men to tend the furnace?"

"Craig found me in the cave, so I decided to learn how the furnace worked while I was down there."

"You went spelunking with bare feet," Sable said incredulously. "Now *that's* what I call macho. No compliment intended."

"None taken. Dillon found the cave door open this morning. I couldn't resist a look."

Sable gave Dillon another pat and turned toward the kitchen. "Did you find out what Simmons was doing on the bus?"

"He says he's going to his mother's funeral."

"Poor Simmons. And now he's stranded."

"Yes," Murph said slowly. "That would be especially hard, since he got on the wrong bus."

Sable's movements stilled.

"Our bus wasn't going to Fayetteville."

"You think Simmons lied?"

"I'm not sure what I think right now," Murph said. "But you may want to avoid being alone with him."

"You're staying in the same room with him."

Murph followed Sable into the kitchen, his bare feet silent on the brick floor. "I'm bigger than you." He walked over to the woodstove. "You know how to cook on this?"

"That depends on what you call cooking. If you mean the act of placing different foods together in a palatable form, all of us could starve while we're waiting for the weather to clear. For breakfast, I'm good at cereal and milk, and maybe scrambled eggs. Home economics was not my favorite class."

"That's okay, as long as you passed science and math."

"Those, I can handle," she said. Her eyes were drawn once again to Murph's bare feet. "How far into the cave did you go?"

"Just back to that ugly-looking pit. I'd imagine you know that cave pretty well."

"Yeah, I've logged quite a few hours down there, exploring passages. Have you been outside?"

"Not yet," he said. "It's like a war zone with all those branches coming down."

"I saw that. I bet the ice is two inches thick on the ground." She took a clean pitcher from the cabinet above the sink, and placed it beneath the spout of the water pump.

"The icicles on the eaves of the house could pass for javelins." Murph grasped the wooden handle, and pumped it up and down. When water trickled from the spout, his eyes widened like those of a child with a new toy. "Hey, this thing really works, doesn't it?"

"Yes, and it's a good thing, because otherwise we'd have to melt ice for water. There's also plenty of food. And do you feel the warmth of the bricks?" She pointed down at the floor. "The furnace is directly below the kitchen."

Murph gave a low whistle of admiration. "Your grandpa knew how to prepare for the worst."

Sable opened the side door of the heavy, cast-iron stove. She struck a match and held it to the papers and kindling wood inside. Flames flickered and spread through the compartment. She tossed the match in and closed the door with a thump.

She opened the refrigerator and took out eggs, sausage and

milk. Everything was still cool, but if the power stayed out, the contents of the fridge would go outside.

Murph picked up a package of sausage and handed it to Sable. "Form this into patties while I mix up a batch of biscuits. Where are the flour and baking things?"

Sable pointed to the proper cupboards, then took the sausage from him with a wry grimace. "You're a cook?"

"My mother was an army cook. You did say there was enough food for everyone."

"There's plenty, believe me. There are always rows of canned goods in the basement. Mom grows a huge garden every year and cans food until it's coming out the eaves of the house. There's flour, sugar, powdered milk in the pantry, and chicken, beef and fish in the freezer. The freezer will keep the meat for several days." Sable formed the first patty and placed it in the hot skillet. The meat sizzled and spattered, sending a smoky aroma through the kitchen.

The first guest soon arrived. It was Audry, her short gray hair combed back from her face in a casual style. She wore a white turtleneck and brown slacks that belonged to Sable's mother.

"They look great on you, Audry," Sable said.

Audry snorted. "Honey, beneath this glamorous exterior lurks the body of a prune. I snooped in your attic this morning. I'm a sneak and an antique freak. Mind if I take another look around later?"

"Of course not. I'm sure the others would like to look for more clothes." As long as they didn't linger up there. Sable had a search to conduct, and she couldn't do it with an audience.

TWELVE

During breakfast, Murph sat at the end of the long, beautifully carved dining table. As he passed the gravy boat, the sausage, the eggs, he studied the others surreptitiously. In the past six weeks he'd been forced to teach himself a few spy techniques. He'd learned to watch people from the periphery of his vision instead of staring straight at them. He'd also learned to tune out chatter, to focus on one conversation—or one voice—at a time.

That was how he overheard Craig telling fifteen-year-old Bryce about all the neat things in the attic, and it was how he overheard Audry remark to Jerri that the biscuits could have used a little more baking soda.

Tomorrow he'd have *her* cook breakfast, if they were all still here. Although, hopefully, she would be gone with the rest of the passengers.

"Delicious biscuits and gravy, Sable," Perry remarked as he selected two more biscuits from the platter.

Sable wrinkled her nose at him. "Murph's the cook. I'm the flunky."

"Many men can cook better than many women." Perry said, splitting open a biscuit. "Look at the great chefs on the cooking channels. They're mainly men. Emeril is my favorite." He raised his fork in the air like a baton. "'Pork fat rules!'"

"I beg your pardon," Audry interjected, "but that kind of fat does not rule, it kills."

"But you must admit, fat adds flavor," Perry argued. "Fat-free cooking just hasn't caught on in America."

"Obviously not for *some* of us," she chided.

Simmons nearly choked on his scrambled eggs.

"That's right," Perry said. "Take it from me, the lard expert. Gaining weight is America's most popular pastime."

Jerri sat down at the other end of the table. "So is that what you packed in that suitcase of yours?" she asked Perry. "That thing has to weigh at least forty pounds."

"Forty-five," Perry said matter-of-factly. "And the contents of my personal luggage are my own business." He broke up a sausage patty and crumbled it atop his biscuit, then spooned a generous dollop of gravy on top of that. "Pork fat *does* rule," he said almost reverently.

He picked up his fork and scooped some of the gravy onto the tines. Like a connoisseur he touched the gravy to his tongue and smacked his lips, inhaling the steam rising from his plate. "Mr. Murphy, my compliments. I must get your recipe before we leave here."

"We'll have time for that," Murph assured him. "Without a thaw, we'll be stuck here for a while."

"Then perhaps I need to check out that attic, myself," Perry said. "I didn't have a change of clothing with me."

"No change of clothes in that case?" Jerri asked.

"It's nothing you need to be concerned about." Perry relished another bite.

They ate in silence for a moment, then Simmons pushed away from the table and picked up his plate.

"Before anyone gets away," Sable said softly, "I need to warn you that we'll need to use the outdoor privy until we get electricity. Our water pump is electric."

Perry's slightly protruding eyes widened. "How far is it from the house?"

"Only about a hundred feet," Sable said.

"In case you hadn't noticed," Perry said, "I'm not elegant on ice."

Simmons snickered. "You're not the one who went over the cliff last night."

Craig stopped eating. "What are you talking about?"

"Sable took a fall," Jerri told him.

"Where?"

"Over the cliffs near the highway," Sable told him.

"If not for the admirable length of my belt," Perry said, "we might not have rescued her."

"Well, hooray for you," Simmons muttered as he left the dining room.

"Is there another way out of here, in case of emergency?" Jerri asked.

"Yes, but it's no better," Craig said. "Sable, you're okay now?"

"I'm fine."

He shook his head and leaned back in his chair. "If I was you, after all you've been through, I'd leave this place and never look back."

Sable took her plate and stood. "I notice *you* haven't left."

Murph got up to help Sable with the dishes.

Craig brought a stack of dishes to the sink. "I need some help chopping wood for the furnace, Murph. Want to join me?"

"I will in a few minutes," Murph told him.

Perry offered to pump water and carry it upstairs.

One by one the others left, until only Murph and Sable remained. They worked for a few moments in silence. Murph had discovered over the past few weeks that he enjoyed working close to Sable.

"Nice little family atmosphere we have, isn't it?" he remarked as peaceful silence enveloped the kitchen.

"Cozy," she drawled. "I'm glad this house is so—"

An angry shout interrupted her. A moment later, Perry burst back through the kitchen door. "Someone has rifled through my suitcase!"

* * *

Sable's tension returned in force. "Was anything missing?"

Perry swallowed and took a deep breath. "No, but my belongings were rearranged. I detest a snoop!"

"Maybe someone was just curious," she soothed. "We *were* discussing the contents of your luggage."

Perry glanced toward the door, then leaned toward them. "Simmons," he muttered. "He left before the rest of us, remember? After all that talk about my heavy suitcase and my…sizable presence, the man decided he could get away with invading my private space. I despise a snoop!"

Audry came rushing into the room, tendrils of gray hair falling across her forehead, face flushed. "Perry Chadwick, what's all the yelling about? I nearly fell down the stairs, you startled me so, hollering and shouting like a house afire."

"Someone searched my suitcase," Perry said. "It was a mess. Nothing was in place."

"So?" Audry said. "My stuff was a mess, too. Even my purse. We were all over that road. Everything shifted."

"Yes, but—"

"Admit it," Audry interrupted, "you hadn't even opened your case until just now."

"Well…I don't think—"

Audry placed a hand on his arm. "I should never have made those comments about your weight, and I apologize. There. I'll take the blame for everything, okay? It's bad enough we're going to be stuck here together for who knows how long, we need to try to cooperate. Come on upstairs and leave poor Sable alone. She's had a rough time of it."

Perry hesitated. He took a deep breath, as if attempting a swift attitude adjustment. He forced a smile that didn't go past the tight corners of his mouth. "Of course you could be right, Audry. I'm sorry I've upset everyone. I suppose I could have jumped to the wrong conclusion. I'm just ill at ease because of the ice storm."

"We're all uncomfortable," Sable said. "Believe me, if I knew a safe way out of here, I'd show it to everyone." And she would feel much safer in the house without these bickering strangers.

"I'm sorry." Perry really did look contrite. He dabbed beads of moisture from his forehead with the back of his hand. "I'm not accustomed to staying in a room with no locks." He paused. "I don't suppose it would be possible for me to move into another room…the attic, perhaps, if there's a lock on the door."

"There isn't, but you can have my room," Sable said. "I'll move a cot—"

"Forget it," Murph said.

"That's right." Audry rested her stern gaze on Perry for a long moment. "I'd be ashamed, asking a young woman to give up her room like that."

"But I didn't—"

"Give it up," Audry insisted. "You're more of a man than that. If you want, you can barricade your door with a chair. I've found that works as well as anything."

Perry gave Sable a look of chagrin, spreading his hands in surrender. "Of course you're right, Audry. How could I be so insensitive?" His voice held a heavy thread of sarcasm. "Sorry, Sable. I was a bit overwrought." He hoisted the band of his pants over his portly belly as he left the room with Audry.

Sable leaned against the counter. Silent questions haunted her, and she turned to find her own uneasiness reflected in Murph's eyes.

"Do you think Audry's right?" she asked.

"It's possible."

"You don't sound convinced. And I didn't imagine being pushed into that ravine."

"I know."

"But I can't be sure it was intentional."

"We need to assume it *was* intentional, and we need to treat Perry's concerns seriously, as well."

"Murph, what are we going to do? We have no phone line to the outside world, no cell reception, not even the radio, since the batteries have died."

"For now, I think we should continue as we are. Maybe that will lure someone into a sense of security. When you're alone in your room, keep the door locked. If we tell the others about what's going on, it'll terrify them, and possibly force someone— whoever it is—to make another move on you."

"Or you, Murph. I was standing right beside you last night. What if you were the intended target?"

"You're Josiah Kessinger's granddaughter."

"But if you're out of the way—"

"We'll both remain watchful."

She gazed out the window at the frozen landscape.

He stepped up behind her. "We're not helpless, Sable. Never forget Who is with us."

"But sometimes I feel I've suddenly been abandoned."

"That won't happen. You belong to Him." He lay a hand on her shoulder. "That's a comfort we both need to remember a little better."

THIRTEEN

The beam of Sable's flashlight made cobwebs glow in the corners of the attic as feminine laughter drifted up from the hallway. Audry and Jerri sat in Jerri's bedroom with the door open, unknowing lookouts. Sable felt secure with them nearby.

This attic was filled with good memories. Tall bureaus, fashionable when Grandpa and Grandma had first bought this place, loomed to the ceiling, sentinels over a collection of other furniture and endless boxes of old clothes.

She remembered being afraid of this place as a small child, until Grandma assured her there was nothing scary up here. Today there were no assurances. Two dear people were already dead, and the reason behind their deaths might lie somewhere in this house, or at least on this property.

"Grandpa, why didn't you talk to me about this?" She gazed around the attic at the boxes of family treasures, pictures, albums, old letters.

She began a search and found tax records, photographs, broken appliances, clothing. And then she opened another box. It held letters from Grandpa to Mom dated last December. Sable took out the contents of one envelope and scanned the pages.

There was nothing new here. He mentioned the buck Boswell had shot on their hunting trip here in November, and how Boswell had gloated about Grandpa falling into a sinkhole and breaking his ankle. He complained about Boswell nagging him to sell the place. For as long as Sable could remember, Boswell had wanted to buy this place. According to Grandpa, he'd increased the pressure since November.

She was returning the letter to its envelope when the bottom step creaked on the attic stairs.

She froze for a second, then realized that Audry and Jerri had fallen silent. When had they stopped their chatter? Had they left the bedroom? Why had she dropped her guard?

She turned off her flashlight and stepped behind a bureau, fighting the panic that shot through her. Someone came slowly—stealthily?—up the staircase. She edged around the bulky bureau and glanced toward the attic steps. They were dark. The intruder wasn't using a flashlight. Why not?

As the form came closer, Sable took an automatic step backward. The floor creaked.

"Who's there?" demanded a familiar male voice. Craig.

Sable started breathing again as she stepped from behind the bureau. "I wish you wouldn't sneak up on people like that." She turned on her flashlight and saw his startled expression.

"Sorry," he muttered.

"Looking for something?" No reason to be afraid of Craig. She needed to stop overreacting.

"I thought I heard someone up here." He came up the last step and ambled toward her, the light from the gable windows casting the dark line of his eyebrows and hair in sharp relief against the winter paleness of his skin.

"I didn't realize I was making noise."

"What're you doing up here in the dark?" he asked.

She replaced the box lid she held. "I turned off my light when I heard you. I didn't know who it was. Instinctive reaction. I always was a little nervous up here alone."

"So why come up here at all?"

"What's it to you? It's *my* family home."

"Whoa. A little cranky, are you?" Craig paced along a row of boxes. He picked up the bowl of an old butter churn. "Your company isn't the most congenial group, is it? That would make me cranky, too. I heard Audry and Perry arguing about his case being searched when I came in from chopping wood."

"Are the limbs still falling like rain?" Sable asked, deliberately changing the subject.

"It's not as bad as it was. Bryce helped some, but I didn't let him stay out long. Murph's out chopping now."

"Where are the others?"

"Bryce is lying in front of the fire with the dog. Audry's examining the antiques in the family room. No telling where Simmons is. Perry's probably in his room, guarding his case." Craig replaced the churn. "You have to admit it's curious. You should have felt that case last night. Heavy. I picked it up once to put it out of the way, and Perry watched me like a mother watching a stranger hold her baby. What do you think he's carrying in that thing?"

"It's none of my business," Sable said. Or was it? "Maybe he's carrying a laptop and doesn't want it stolen."

"A forty-five pound laptop? Get real, Sable." Craig's eyes flashed with curiosity. "Like you said, it's your home. I'd watch everybody a little closer."

Sable dusted her hands together and bent over another box.

"Uh, Sable?" Craig took a slow step closer to her.

She glanced at him over her shoulder.

"Is something wrong?" he asked.

"What do you mean?"

He stepped around a box. His candid brown eyes narrowed. "Why did you turn around and come straight back home? You've had a wreck, you nearly died on the cliff this morning, and today you're as jumpy as a buck during hunting season. Is it money?"

"Money?"

"Look, I know this place cost a lot of money to fix up, and it's not bringing in any income since it isn't being farmed anymore." He hesitated, glancing around the attic. "I wasn't going to bring this up yet, but...well...when your family decides to sell, I want to be first on the list, before you call a Realtor."

"Sell?"

Craig cleared his throat. "Now, don't turn me down just like that. I have more money than you think. The boat dock brings in a good living. My expenses aren't much, and I've stuck a lot in the bank. Enough to pay half down on the asking price."

"Asking price? Craig, Grandpa's not even cold in the grave yet, and you're already after his property?"

"Hey, don't get mad. I just offered to buy the place, not burn it down. My parents got an offer for their property—they need the money to help fund Dad's campaign. I've always liked this place. You know that."

She straightened to scan the rear wall with her flashlight beam. "You sound like Otis Boswell—or didn't you know he was trying to buy Grandpa out, too?"

There was a long silence, and she turned to look at Craig, whose brows had drawn together in a scowl. "Josiah didn't sell, did he? Not to that goon."

"No, but do you have any good reasons why we shouldn't? Boswell's got the funds."

"Filthy money."

"I know you have personal grievances against him," she said. "I've just never known why."

Craig looked at her for a moment in the dim light, then sighed and stepped over to the dormer window. He stood looking outside for a long moment. Sable had almost concluded the conversation had ended when he turned around.

"Dad's running for state senator, you know."

"What does he have to do with Otis Boswell?"

Craig shoved his hands into the pockets of his jeans, and turned to stare out the window again. "Dad's a good man."

She softened her voice. "I know he is. He's always been a good neighbor, and he'll be a great senator."

Craig hesitated again. "How…how loyal are you to Otis Boswell?"

"I'm not."

"Are you going back to Oklahoma?"

She relented slightly. "No, Craig. I want to come back here

to live. With Grandpa gone, there's nothing for me in Freemont."
Except arrest, maybe.

Craig looked toward the stairs, then leaned closer to her. "We've been friends a long time, right?" There was a vulnerability in his deep voice that touched her.

"Of course."

He paused and took a breath. "Remember when Jimmy Ray and I were in the car accident that killed Tom Hall?"

"How could I forget something like that? You were a senior in high school. I was in my first year at Columbia."

He grimaced, looking at the floor. "My blood alcohol was one point five."

"You were *drunk?*"

"Yes, but Tom swerved into my lane—all the way over. I didn't want to hit him head-on, and I couldn't pull off the road because it was on the bridge at Eagle Rock, remember?"

"So you traded lanes with him. I know all this. But, Craig, you were drunk?"

"He swerved back at the last second. That's really what happened, Sable. It wasn't my fault, but that didn't matter. All the authorities focused on was the alcohol. I was eighteen. I could have been tried as an adult for manslaughter."

That would have been tragic. She knew it. Craig hadn't been a bad kid, just restless at times.

"Dad was a judge then," Craig said. "He pulled a lot of strings with his friends to keep me out of big trouble."

"So you're saying your father used his political influence to prevent you from being prosecuted?" She heard judgment in her words and voice, felt the hard knot that tightened in her stomach.

"I'm sorry," he said. "You can't imagine how sorry. I shouldn't have been drinking, I know that. I'll live with it the rest of my life, and believe me, it isn't easy. But I do remember the circumstances of the wreck, and I didn't cause it. You have to understand why Dad did what he did."

"I understand he didn't trust the judicial system he'd sworn to uphold." She hated the harshness in her voice. Hated that she was taking her pent-up bitterness out on Craig because of everything else that was happening.

"He didn't want his son to go to prison."

"So that makes it right?" *Stop, Sable! Stop it.*

"Dad doesn't make a habit of it. If I'd been caught joyriding in a stolen car, or shoplifting, or driving under the influence, he'd have let me take my knocks, but this was different. You can see that, can't you?"

If it had happened to one of her brothers, no one would have pulled any strings for either of them. But she knew Craig was living with a lot of regret.

"Dad stuck his neck out," Craig said. "He laid his whole career on the line for me. He almost lost it, thanks to Otis Boswell."

"What happened?" She resigned herself to hear the dirty details.

"Jimmy Ray's father couldn't keep his mouth shut. He went fishing with Otis one day, and told Otis what Dad did. A couple of years later, Otis had a chance to buy some private property in the middle of the Mark Twain National Forest. He petitioned for some zoning changes so he could set up a galena mine on the property, but his petition was blocked. He went to Dad and threatened to expose me if Dad didn't pull some strings."

"And your father gave in?"

Craig closed his eyes and nodded. "He didn't think he had a choice. It didn't work, anyway. The land suddenly went off the market, and Otis went to Oklahoma."

Sable leaned against the window frame as she digested this information. "You mean Otis had reason to believe there was galena around here?"

"That's right," Craig said. He turned and started for the stairs. "I've got wood to chop. If you change your mind about selling, let me know."

Sable listened to the sound of his descending footsteps, angry with herself for her behavior. Why couldn't she have just listened to Craig's story without hurling blame at him? He was baring his soul—risking his reputation and his father's—to warn her about Otis Boswell.

Maybe she should pay more attention to the warning—and lighten up on the judgment.

She leaned forward and pressed her forehead against the cold glass of the dormer window. "Oh, Grandpa, why?"

A movement outside caught her attention, and she saw Murph several hundred feet away, splitting wood beside the creek. She recognized his size and the breadth of his shoulders. He raised the ax high into the air and plunged it into a log in a perfect split. Two more strikes, and he moved to the next log.

She enjoyed watching him work, and she was so grateful for his presence here. Until the sun broke through, or until the temperature warmed, the ground would remain encrusted with ice and all of the bus passengers would remain stranded.

Impatient with her own thoughts, she studied the thick barrier of clouds that had settled over the hills. The atmosphere in the house seemed to reflect the sky.

When she looked back down into the woods, she was surprised to see another figure moving through the trees above the place where Murph was working.

Murph handled the ax as if it were a lightweight toy, breaking away ice with a flick of his arm. The newcomer balanced on a cliff above Murph, in a thicket of tangled brush so dense Sable could barely make out the human form. At times the figure was barely visible, at times merely a part of the dark green line of cedar trees near the ledge—except for a bright, red-orange halo that seemed to bob with the person's movements. A knit cap?

Something about this intruder grabbed Sable's attention, something stealthy, as if…as if he were trying—

Sable gasped. "No!"

The figure raised a branch the size of a man's leg, moving into a line above Murph.

Sable unlocked the window and shoved it up. She fumbled with the lever of the storm window, tried to open it. It wouldn't move.

She pounded on the window. "Murph!" She looked around for something to hurl through the glass, fumbled once more at the window frame and felt it give. She shoved it hard, and as the pane flew up she cried, "Murph! Watch out!"

The assailant heaved the branch over the cliff at Murph.

At the sound of her voice, Murph straightened and looked around. The branch hit the side of his head, then crashed to the ground. Murph plunged face-first across a half-cut log.

FOURTEEN

Sable raced downstairs from the attic to the living room, flung open the front door and rushed out into the icy air, stopping only when she reached the slick steps that led down from the front porch to the yard. She grabbed the pickax someone had leaned against the steps and used it to balance herself across the frozen slope.

There was no longer any doubt, someone had tried to kill Murph—and may have succeeded! Someone had come stalking, and he or she was in these woods, right now.

Sable scrambled across the ice to a steep, old trail a couple hundred feet from the house. She raised the pickax over her head and plunged the tip through the thick ice crust, pulling herself up a few feet at a time, frustrated by the slow progress. When she reached level ground again, she scrambled through the trees toward the place she had seen Murph fall.

"Murph!" She grabbed at the slender trunk of a dogwood to keep her balance. "Murph, answer me!" She couldn't see him.

A crash reached her from a stand of cedars, a crackle of brush and the tinkle of ice—the attacker was getting away. She couldn't take time to follow.

At last, just past a huge, bare-branched oak, she caught a glimpse of Murph's tan coat. His limp body lay over the log where he had fallen, the ax beside him in the ice.

Sable rushed toward him, using the pickax. "Murph, please answer me!" Sharp spines of a cedar branch slapped her face.

Murph groaned. Which meant he had an airway and was breathing.

She stumbled to his side. "Murph, can you hear me?"

Again, he groaned and started to turn over.

"Don't move. Not yet. You know the drill. Wiggle your fingers."

He did. All moved well. "I'm okay," he said. "Now can I move?" His speech wasn't slurred.

She grabbed his arm and helped him turn over. A red welt followed the line of his right cheek and the right side of his neck. Several small cuts seeped blood. He opened his eyes. His pupils were equal and reactive.

"Thank God you're alive," she said.

"I'm not sure I'm ready to be thankful for that yet," he muttered under his breath.

"Tell me what day of the week it is."

"Saturday afternoon, we arrived earlier this morning in the middle of an ice storm, your birthday is next week, and you'll be thirty-one. Satisfied?"

"You can sit up. Slowly."

He blinked and raised his head. "Man, I didn't hear that coming." He sat up, grimacing. "Should've waited for Craig to help. Dangerous under these trees."

Sable darted a glance up the cliff, where she had seen the other figure. "The branch didn't fall."

"What?"

"Somebody threw that limb at you from the top of that cliff." She pointed to where crevassed rocks loomed overhead, then to the log a few feet away. "If you hadn't moved when you did, you'd have a crushed skull."

His face gradually lost its color, and Sable braced herself against him. "Murph, rest for a moment. I can't hold you, and you can't afford another fall."

He touched the side of his face, then turned his head from side to side. "I'll be okay. Did you see who it was?"

"All I saw was a shadow of green topped by red. Most likely a stocking cap. Did you hear me shout from the window?"

"Yes. That's why I turned." He took her hand. "That was a close one. If you hadn't called to me, I might be dead. Did you see who was in the house as you left?"

"No. I'm sorry. I was so panicked when I ran out of the house, I didn't think to pay any attention. I didn't tell anybody, I just ran." She shivered. "Oh, Murph, I was so scared. All I could think about was reaching you. I—"

He placed his fingers gently on her lips. "You did fine."

Sable shivered again.

"You're terrified." His fingers trailed across her face, and he cupped her chin. "You didn't even stop to get a coat." He undid the buttons of his thick, quilted jacket.

"I'll be okay. Let's get back to the house."

"We will, but first…" He pulled the jacket from his shoulders and placed it around hers. The lingering warmth from his body encompassed her. "If you must rescue me, allow me to salvage some of my macho pride with a gesture of chivalry."

She accepted the coat. "I'll be glad to help. But let me complete my mission. You need some medical attention, and that's back at the house."

"Agreed. And now I'm cold." He bent to pick up his ax, and he stumbled.

She grabbed his arm. "Are you okay?"

He retrieved the ax and straightened up. "I'll be fine, just a little dizzy when I bend over."

"Then don't bend over."

The fine lines around his eyes deepened with amusement. He looked down at her as he put an arm across her shoulders. "It's nice to know you're so concerned, Doc. Think we can get back to the house without another fall?"

"If we walk in the brush and dried grass to the side of the trail, it isn't quite as bad."

"Good observation." He stepped into the patches of broken

ice where Sable had used her pickax, and together they made their way back toward the house. Slowly.

"Murph, I've been talking with Craig, and a lot of things have fallen into place. Boswell has resorted to blackmail in the past to get what he wanted."

"How does Craig know about it?"

Sable hesitated. "His father was the one blackmailed."

"Why am I not surprised?"

They stepped out of the woods and crossed the frozen yard toward the house. The house was constructed of brick, with white columns supporting the front porch, and black shutters at each window. Today, all the shutters were folded back, and the blinds were raised to let in as much light as possible. This gave the unfortunate impression of eyes open wide, watching every move Sable and Murph made.

"You could hike out of this hollow with a pickax, the way you hiked to me," Murph said. "Get help from a neighbor."

"The neighbors are in the same situation."

"Call for help."

"From where? The neighbors won't have cell reception, either. Our radio doesn't work. The battery's dead. The lines are down all over with this kind of ice. Face it, Murph, we're stranded."

Murph had trouble concentrating as he stepped onto the front porch—partly because his brains had a tendency to scramble lately when he was near Sable, but mostly because of the pain that shot through his head and down his neck with persistent frequency.

He decided he had a great deal in common with Josiah Kessinger—he felt an instinctive need to protect Sable, and in doing so he had downplayed his fear. Whoever had tried to kill him may be—probably was—planning to kill Sable after she led the way to the object—or objects—of this treasure hunt. If she didn't realize this yet, she would soon.

When they stepped through the front door, Audry greeted them from the sofa.

"At last," she said, getting up. "For a while, I thought I'd been deserted. Where is everyone?"

"I don't know about the others," Murph said, "but we were out in the—"

"Murph!" The older woman rushed toward him, reaching up to touch the side of his face. "What on earth happened to you?"

Murph winced and stepped back. "A limb hit me. I'll live."

"A limb? I knew it would happen. These storms are deadly. We need to get some ice on that right away. I'll get a dish towel and some ice. I'll be right back—"

"Audry," Sable interrupted, "was anyone else outside recently? We wouldn't want more injuries."

"Nobody I know of," Audry said. "It's a pretty sure bet Perry wouldn't try it. He barely made it to the outdoor privy this afternoon. Took him thirty minutes to get there and back, and I saw him fall twice. I think he's taking a nap now. He has decided to haul water for the indoor facilities."

"And Simmons?" Murph asked.

Audry shrugged. "Haven't seen him, don't want to."

Before Murph could ask about Craig, the basement door opened and Craig stepped through it. He switched off his flashlight and set it on the shelf behind the door. "The wood furnace is filled," he said. "To capacity. How'd you do out there, Murph? Do we have enough wood to last us a few days?"

Murph paused. "Not as much—"

"Man, can't you see he's wounded?" Audry exclaimed. "Anybody who goes outside ought to wear a helmet. Surely you can make what we have last until the ice stops breaking the branches."

Craig's surprise and concern appeared genuine to Murph, but there was no time to think about it before the door to the family room opened across the hallway from the kitchen.

Bryce ambled out with a book in his hand. "Hey, Sable, can I borrow this? There's no electricity for a TV or computer, and I'm getting bored."

Sable stopped to talk to him, and Murph followed Audry into

the kitchen before anyone else could ask questions about his injury. He needed to be the one asking questions. He needed to know where the others had been while he was being bashed in the head.

FIFTEEN

Firelight flickered against the paneled walls with a muted glow. Usually at this time on sunny afternoons, the light filtering through the long bay window embraced the pastel floral colors of sofa, chairs and drapes that Sable had chosen so carefully last summer. All looked gray today.

Sable turned from the window to the fire. The sounds of chatter and laughter drifted from the family room, where Audry, Jerri and Bryce played a spirited card game. Murph was upstairs lying down.

The guests had been scattered throughout the house when Murph was attacked; no one had seen a thing.

Even the colors worn by Murph's attacker gave Sable no clue—there were always two or three green coveralls and a couple of red knit caps in the mudroom, used often by the family in the wintertime. Murph's assailant had obviously found the mudroom.

Murph had left firm orders for Sable to stay near the others, and if she couldn't do that, to keep Dillon with her. Sable, in turn, had given firm orders for him to rest, and to let her know immediately if he noticed any changes in his vision, any dizziness or worsening of pain. He knew the routine. She had checked on him twenty minutes ago.

Simmons was in the dining room with a cup of coffee and a back copy of *Field & Stream*. Craig had gone back outside to round up more wood, in spite of Audry's dire warnings of the dangers involved.

Dillon lay at the hearth, his ears pricking forward every time someone stepped through the living room.

Sable paced through the living room and paused at the old rock collection on a low shelf beside the staircase.

Before he married, Grandpa had traveled extensively throughout the United States, hitching rides on boxcars. His stories about the places he'd visited and this small display of stones was all that remained from his travels.

Sable knew the shape and color of every mineral specimen, and the story that went with each. By the time she was ten, she had known as much about Grandpa's collection as he knew himself. Something had seemed odd to her last night when she glanced at the shelf, and now, as she studied the collection, she realized that some of the mineral chunks had been disturbed.

She picked up a lump of coal Grandpa had carried from Pennsylvania and studied the position of the rose quartz. Hadn't there been a chunk of galena between them? The galena was now where the sphalerite used to be. Sable had never labeled them because she had known them by heart. But now…

"That dog seems to like you." Audry's voice drifted quietly from the hallway.

Sable turned from the display case. "I like him, too."

The older woman's sherry-brown eyes filled with sympathy as she ambled toward the sofa. "Sable, I was so sorry to hear about your grandfather. We haven't had much time alone to talk. Would it be too intrusive to ask what caused his death?"

"He was in an automobile accident."

"I'm so sorry."

Both women turned as Perry Chadwick thumped heavily down the steps. He wore a tan dress shirt and a pair of slightly wrinkled brown slacks. His thin, pale brown hair clung to his scalp, and the scant light from the window revealed a red blotch on the second fold of his triple chin.

"You're going to have a nasty bruise there," Audry said. "You should have let me put a vinegar poultice on that place."

"What happened?" Sable asked.

"I fell on the way to the outdoor privy," Perry said. "Which is why I'm carrying water to the bathrooms."

"He can't stay on his feet long enough to get wood from the porch into the house," Audry said. "Perry, you're just not coordinated. If you'd gone to help chop in the forest, they'd have had to carry you back on a stretcher."

Perry nodded. "It's the feet, you know. They aren't big enough to balance the weight of my body." He grimaced. "That may change if we're here for long. I've been looking over the food supplies."

"Naturally," Audry said.

"Lots of good canned stuff, lots of meat." Perry shook his head. "But there are quite a few people in this house, and we don't know how long we'll be here."

"We aren't going to starve," Audry said.

"Speak for yourself," Perry protested. "You don't need as much fuel to keep you alive. This may be the diet of all diets."

While the two exchanged mild barbs, Sable thought again about the case that Perry had guarded with such fierceness, and wondered what might be inside.

Perry gave up the argument and strolled toward the kitchen.

Audry chuckled as he disappeared. "He reminds me of my grandson, the rascal. Always hanging around the kitchen underfoot. I took the liberty of preparing some stew this afternoon, and every time Perry returned for more water, he had to sample the food, offer suggestions for seasoning, make a nuisance of himself. He can be amusing when he isn't busy worrying about that silly suitcase of his."

"I'm glad somebody has a good attitude about all this," Sable said. "I'm also glad he's carrying the water. That's quite a job. I wouldn't want it."

"You're in good physical condition, you don't need help getting into shape."

Sable considered the older woman's slender, wiry form. "You're in pretty good shape, yourself."

"I try to keep toned. Time to check up on Perry. Can't let him ruin dinner—or eat it all up."

Sable waited until she heard Audry and Perry bantering in the kitchen, then she glanced up the stairs. She had a crazy thought that wouldn't go away: What would a snoop have found in Perry's suitcase?

It was none of her business, and Perry was barely able to navigate outside, much less possess the nimble precision it would take to hover over a cliff edge and target Murph's head with a limb. If he had been the one to push her last night, he would most likely have fallen with her.

But what if he was faking? She couldn't avoid the questions. What could be so important to Perry that he would lug a heavy suitcase all the way here last night and protect it as if it were precious cargo? He'd had other luggage on the bus, and yet he had chosen the one piece that had contained no change of clothes.

The rise and fall of the voices in the kitchen told her Audry and Perry were still embroiled in their good-natured bickering. The others, except for Murph, were either downstairs or outside. If she wanted to snoop, this was the time. She gestured silently for Dillon to follow her.

The sewing room occupied by Perry was down the hall, right of the staircase, directly across from the room Murph and Simmons were sharing. The sewing room had two tall, wide windows that allowed a surprising amount of light through, considering that the room faced the mountainside.

Sable opened the door and glanced in. She hesitated. The case was surely locked, especially since Perry was convinced someone had broken into it this morning. Still…she took a step forward.

The door across the hallway opened suddenly. She stiffened as icy needles of tension shot beneath her skin.

"Doing some dusting?" came Paul Murphy's wry voice.

She sagged against the doorjamb with relief. "It's no use, I can't do this. It's crazy."

"Dusting is crazy?" He came closer.

"I was going to find out what's in Perry's overnight case," she whispered, turning to check the injury on his face. For the amount of abuse his face and neck had sustained, he looked surprisingly good.

"That isn't an overnight case, it's a steamer trunk," Murph said. "Don't let me stop you. I'd like to see for myself what's inside."

"Then feel free to go on in. I was just chickening out. Remember how Perry said he hates snoops?"

Murph opened the door wider, coming so close she could feel the caress of his breath against her forehead. "We're both in on this one," he said. "After you."

Sable hesitated. Much as she hated to admit it, she didn't feel quite so nervous with Murph along. "But should we be doing this?" she asked.

"We're not stealing anything, we're trying to protect ourselves from being murdered. I've tossed etiquette out the window." He turned to Dillon. "Stay and watch, boy. Warn us if anyone starts up the stairs."

The German shepherd sat.

Sable checked the upstairs landing once more, then quickly stepped into the room. "Perry will have a seizure if he catches us. You saw how angry he was earlier."

"That's why this is a good idea. What's so important about that suitcase? Why was he so concerned about its contents? When I borrowed some toiletry supplies from Craig, he told me Perry had asked to use them, too. So what's in the case?"

They saw a laptop on the cot. That would account for five or six pounds. Sable found the suitcase beneath the cot. She tugged at the handle to pull it out, and lost her grip. "Wow. That thing is heavy."

Murph reached down, pulled out the oblong, hard-sided black case, and set it on the thin mattress beside the laptop.

"Can you pick locks?" Sable asked.

"Yes, but first let's try the old-fashioned approach." He pushed against the metal latches and they snapped open.

Sable stared at it.

"Now who's the pessimist?" Murph teased. He lifted the lid of the case to reveal the colorful—and heavy—contents.

Nestled in the old, worn suitcase that Perry Chadwick had carried so protectively in the ice storm, were several volumes of books with pictures of food on their covers.

"Cookbooks!" Sable exclaimed.

Murph pulled out a large hardback. "Betty Crocker."

"Cookbooks," Sable said.

Murph chuckled.

"Shh!" She picked up another heavy tome. "Master Chefs. At least we know Audry wasn't the one who snooped earlier. She won't let Perry near the food." Anxious to retreat, Sable replaced everything as she'd found it and closed the case.

Murph lifted it and placed it back beneath the cot. "Let's get out of here."

Sable hurried out into the hallway with Murph. She walked toward the window at the end of the hallway while Murph closed the door behind them and joined her. Even in the dim light she could see the deep red mark at the side of his face.

Without thinking she reached up and gently touched the swollen welt. "How do you feel?"

His jaw tensed.

"I'm sorry, I know it hurts."

A comfortable smile spread across his face. "You've got the healing touch, Doc. I think I'm going to live."

"If I thought otherwise I wouldn't have let you out of my sight."

His smile widened. "Speaking of which, I don't think I've thanked you for saving my life."

"You're welcome, but you're still one up on me. You've rescued me twice now. Have I told you I'm scared?"

He put his hands on her shoulders. "Of course we're afraid.

It means we're sane." He moved his hands to the base of her neck and massaged it in slow, easy movements. "I don't see anything wrong with fearing for our lives."

Instead of relaxing her, his touch sent warning signals to every nerve in her body. A different kind of danger. She stepped aside.

Reluctantly, he released her. "Don't trust me, either?"

"I don't want to complicate an already complicated mess."

"Who's complicating things? Your neck muscles are really—"

"Would you stop it?" In spite of her tension, she couldn't prevent a smile. Paul Murphy was an easy man to like. "I'm sorry, Murph."

"Sorry about what?" He didn't move away, and he silently drew her gaze, though he didn't touch her again.

"I'm sorry that I'm not eager to become involved in more than one dangerous situation at a time."

He chuckled. "I'm not that dangerous."

"But fear can trigger emotional impulses one wouldn't ordinarily have, and those can lead to wrong decisions."

"So if I understand what you're saying," Murph said, "you're afraid that, if our friendship were to grow into something more, I would suddenly become a threat to you in some way?"

"You're twisting my words. I just think we need to get through this situation alive without allowing attraction to cloud our judgment."

He inclined his head. "That makes sense. We'll get through this situation."

Sable turned and walked toward the stairs.

"Afterward, we can concentrate on the romance," he added.

"That isn't what I meant."

Murph caught up with her, and once more stopped just short of enfolding her in his arms. "So what did you mean?"

She turned to look up at him, and felt her pulse quicken at the serious expression in his eyes. This was no light flirtation; he meant business. But so did she.

"I love my career and my independence. I'm sorry, but I have to make this clear. I saw my grandparents fight often because Grandma ran her own restaurant in Eureka Springs. She worked long hours, and came home cranky, and she and Grandpa hardly ever saw eye to eye. I don't think it works to combine a career with a romance."

"Sorry, but as trite as it may sound, your actions speak a different language."

She scowled. "You could be reading my actions in the wrong way. I'm a doctor. If you're referring to my so-called healing touch, I try to do that with all my patients."

"Seems to me I've picked up on a little more than professional interest," he said.

"You don't have a problem with self-confidence, do you?"

"Actually," he said, then paused thoughtfully, "when it comes to you, I feel extremely insecure, but with something that could become important to both of us, I think it would be a mistake to turn tail and run."

She blinked in surprise. Transparent honesty? Wow.

"Besides which," he continued, "come to think of it, you did tell me, in so many words, how concerned you were about my welfare. Remember? Up on the hill?" He gingerly touched the welt on his cheek. "I think I can take that personally."

"You're too pushy, Paul Murphy. It could land you in trouble someday."

To her surprise, she caught a glint of amusement in his expression. Feeling a sudden, inexplicable smile attempting to take over her face, she swung back toward the staircase.

"Wait a minute, where are you going?" he asked.

"Downstairs to check on the food. I'm cold and hungry, and arguing with you isn't helping."

"If it's okay with you, I'd like to look around the attic. I know you said your grandfather put all his important things in an impenetrably locked safe, but it doesn't hurt to keep trying. Maybe I can even figure out the combination."

Sable hesitated.

"Do you need me to come downstairs with you for some reason?" he asked.

"No, I just…"

His expression changed, and all the teasing lightness in his eyes vanished. "You don't trust me alone in the attic."

"I trust you, but you could be attacked up there as easily as you were attacked outside."

"Oh." Some of the lightness returned. "Then keep watch. Everyone is downstairs, right? Make sure they stay there. And keep Dillon with you." He gave her a reassuring smile. "I'll see you later."

She watched as he padded up the attic steps in his stocking feet, then she went downstairs. Every time she was with Murph she felt as if tiny fibers of friendship, mutual support and attraction were drawing them closer. This was the worst possible time to consider a relationship. And yet…Paul Murphy was a hard man to put out of her mind.

When she reached the display case with the rock collection downstairs, she studied the specimens again. Nothing was missing, just rearranged. The chunks of galena and sphalerite—the only specimens Grandpa had collected from his own cave—were still there.

"I've been meaning to ask you about that stuff," a voice came from behind.

Sable started and swung around to see Jerri coming toward her from the direction of the family room. Jerri had short, curly hair the color of sweet potatoes, streaked blond at the temples. She was slightly shorter than Sable but weighed about forty pounds more—mostly muscle.

"Sorry, I didn't mean to sneak up on you." Jerri's voice was low and melodious. "Craig told me a little about how your grandfather went around collecting all these rocks. He sounds like an interesting man."

"He was."

"Craig sure has a thing for all this stuff. He told me about the different stones and the minerals they contain."

"Craig's a spelunker and amateur rock hound from childhood. He knows these hills better than I do."

"He's smart, all right," Jerri said. "Never thought a plain old rock could be so interesting." She paused and winked. "Of course, that might have something to do with who's talking. But really, Sable, are any of these pieces worth anything?"

"Only memories." Sable picked up a geode and watched the sparkles inside the hollow rock reflect light from the room.

"So that story about the history of this place was just a story?"

"No, it was true enough. I mean, those two partners actually did own this place, and they did disappear. But as for the silver, you know how rumors get started. Someone probably found a piece of galena down in the cave and jumped to conclusions."

"Must've been somebody who didn't know much about minerals. Even I know what galena looks like, all boxy, straight sides." She indicated the piece of galena on the shelf.

"Really?" Sable said. "Not a lot of people know the difference. Are you interested in geology?"

"I'm interested in a little of everything, especially when Craig Holt is doing the talking." She grinned. "Maybe those partners started the rumor about silver so they could sell the cave for a profit."

Sable winced at the words. Was that really what Grandpa had done with the Seitz mine? "That's a thought."

"Good as any, huh? Wonder how dinner's coming. I'm getting hungry. Think I'll go take a look."

Sable watched Jerri leave, then turned back to the case, hating the suspicions that persisted in her mind, hating her jumpy nerves every time someone spoke to her.

Audry poked her head out of the kitchen door. "Food's ready as soon as Murph and Craig and Simmons come in."

"Simmons? I thought he was in the dining room."

"His jacket wasn't on the hall tree. He must have gone outside."

"Okay, Audry. I'll wash, then go find them if I can." She called Dillon to follow her upstairs.

The moment she stepped into her bedroom, Dillon growled behind her.

She froze on the threshold. "What?"

He brushed past her, obviously on alert, his legs stiff, the fur of his ruff prickling upward. He sniffed the comforter.

"No, wait. Dillon, get back." What if someone was in here under the bed or in the closet or even hiding in the cedar chest? "Let's get out of here."

SIXTEEN

Murph was descending the last of the squeaky attic steps, brushing cobwebs from his arms and shoulders, when Sable appeared in the entryway, blue eyes wide.

"Dillon thinks someone's been in my room," she said.

"I'll check it out. You stay here." Instinctively, Murph reached beneath his shirt and freed the Detonics from its holster, wishing he had informed Sable earlier about the loaded weapon he carried. Now there was no time.

She gasped when she caught sight of the pistol.

"Stay here." He gripped the gun in both hands and crept down the hallway. Dillon followed, his growls still rumbling. When they reached the open door, Murph paused and listened.

He heard only the chatter of voices downstairs, and Sable's frightened breathing behind him…directly behind him.

"I thought I told you to stay put," he muttered.

"Is anyone in the room?"

"I don't know yet." He allowed Dillon to enter first.

The dog growled softly as he approached the cedar chest. He sniffed it thoroughly, then followed a scent to the straight-backed chair beside the antique chest of drawers. He didn't growl this time, but sniffed at the drawer handles.

"I don't think anyone's here now." Still, Murph entered carefully, arms braced. He crept to the closet, opened the door. No one.

He stepped over to the cedar chest and lifted the lid. Nothing.

With one foot, he raised the dust ruffle of the bed and peered underneath. "I think it's clear."

Sable came in behind him. "But someone's been here." She gestured toward the cedar chest. "This has been moved away from the bed. I know, because I tried to pull the comforter up last night and it was tucked between the chest and the bed frame." She checked the closet and the bureau drawers.

"Is anything missing?" Murph asked.

She shuffled through a stack of folded underwear. "The letter is missing." She looked up at him. "The one Grandpa wrote to Mom that we read last night."

"Not the confession note?" Murph asked.

She patted her pocket. "I have it here. But I put the other letter in this drawer this morning when I dressed, and it's gone. Obviously, Perry wasn't imagining things. I wonder if the other rooms have been searched."

Murph engaged the safety of his pistol.

"Paul, where did you get that gun?"

"I've carried it with me since I arrived in Freemont."

She sank onto the bed. "It's yours?"

"Of course it's mine. I'll explain later. Right now we have more important things to discuss." He reached into the pocket of his jeans and pulled out a three-inch by four-inch photograph. He held it to the light from the window. "Recognize any of these people?"

Her interest focused. "That looks like a really old picture of Grandpa and Otis Boswell, and…the woman? Audry?"

"I thought so, too."

She took the picture from him and carried it to the window, held it to the light. The woman's hair was dark, cut in a pageboy, a few tendrils fanning across a very attractive face. "It is her."

"But this had to be taken thirty-five or forty years ago," he said.

"She told us herself she once lived in Eagle Rock. She knows this area. Remember?"

"But why didn't she say anything about knowing Josiah?"

"There could be any number of reasons."

"What's your first guess?" he asked.

"Obviously I'm suspicious. It could be she either knows something she doesn't want to talk about, or she's still connected to Boswell in some way."

Sable stepped away from the window. Dillon paced along beside her, a loving, protective shadow. She stopped in front of Murph and looked up at him. "I think I'd better have a talk with her."

"What if the outrageous is true and she's our stalker? Shouldn't we treat this as just more evidence, and keep our mouths shut for now?"

Sable studied the photograph a moment longer, then handed it back to Murph, pointing at the proprietary hand Audry had on Grandpa's arm. "What does that look like to you?"

"Don't jump to conclusions, Sable," he said gently.

She turned away, and her hand reached up and grasped the old pocket watch that hung from a chain around her neck. Her fingers rubbed across the smooth metal.

"You're always doing that." Murph gestured to her hand. "Reaching up for it, as if it reassures you. I'm curious why Josiah would give you a watch that didn't work. I know it's a keepsake, but surely it wouldn't be too expensive to replace the mechanism inside." Murph reached out and fingered the delicate design of the watch, then took it in his hand and tested the weight. "I wonder…I'd've expected Josiah Kessinger to have this watch repaired before he gave it to you, unless there was some reason he couldn't."

She turned the watch over. "He had it engraved."

Murph read the words on the smooth metal. "'To Sable with love. A treasure for a treasure.'" He smiled at the sentiment. "Maybe I'm just grasping at straws right now. Maybe that bump on the head affected me more than I thought, but have you checked the inner workings?"

"I never thought—"

"Now might be a good time to look."

She slipped the chain over her head. "I just took it for granted Grandpa was giving this to me because it had been so much a part of him, and he knew I loved it."

"But it wasn't working when he gave it to you."

"No, and it had always worked before. I remember what he said when he gave it to me, too, because at the time it sounded kind of strange. He said, 'You may need it someday, punkin. I know all I have to.' But I wondered what he meant." She tried to twist the back plate without result. "Do you have a pocketknife?"

Murph pulled one out, opened it, handed it to her. "Wouldn't hurt to check."

She slipped the point of the blade into the tiny groove between the back plate and the body of the watch. With care, she pried at the plate until it slipped into her hand.

A square of thin, white paper was stuffed into the casing where the inner workings of the watch had once been. Sable used the knife to pry this out, as well.

Murph barely caught the small, shiny nugget that fell from the folds of paper.

"Galena?" Sable asked, reaching for the nugget. She caught her breath when he dropped it into her hand. "That isn't galena. That's…it looks more like…"

She grabbed the paper from Murph and unfolded it quickly, tearing off a corner in her haste. She scanned the page quickly. "Murph, this is a metallurgist's assay sheet for a sample of high-grade silver," she whispered.

"From where?"

"I don't know."

"You sure Josiah never said a word about this?"

"Don't you think I'd remember something like that?" She held the nugget to the murky light from the window.

"Could it be on this place somewhere?" Murph asked.

Sable looked up at him. "As far as I know, there's never been silver found in this part of Missouri before, especially not a vein of high-grade silver like this."

"Could that story about the cave be true?" Murph asked.

"You're the second person to ask me that in the past twenty minutes."

"Could it have something to do with your grandfather's death?"

The words fell between them like chips of ice, solid with frightening possibilities.

"I don't know what to think right now," she whispered.

Murph refolded the analysis sheet with the silver and stuffed it back inside the watch. He took the back plate and snapped it on. "There's still not enough evidence to do more than guess. The best place for this is where it's always been." He slipped the chain over her head, then smoothed a tendril of soft black hair from her face. He wished he could smooth all her heartache away, protect her from all harm and prove that the world wasn't really as frightening as it looked right now.

He could only pray that God would. "Meanwhile, stay close to me," he told her. "If you find something even remotely questionable, tell me immediately." His fingers caressed her soft cheek, and then, as if he couldn't help himself, he allowed a featherlight touch along her neck to rest against the beating pulse at her throat. "Your heart's racing."

"Of course it's racing. I'm scared."

"Me, too."

"Murph, if you can have a gun, I want to carry one, too. There's an old .22 pistol down the hall in the closet. My brothers and I used it for target practice. I'm going to—"

"I don't think that's a good idea."

"Why not? You're carrying one, and you've obviously been carrying it for some time. If you can have a concealed weapon, why can't I?"

"You don't have a license. I do."

This bit of news obviously surprised her, but she recovered quickly. "Are you an undercover cop or something?"

"No. I had to work a job out of the country for a while, and I was required to carry this for protection."

She crossed her arms over her chest. "You know, Murph, your

macho attitude is getting on my nerves just a little. Grandpa would have been proud, but I'm not impressed."

In spite of the serious circumstances, Murph felt a grin spread across his face, and he couldn't stop it. He saw Sable's eyes narrow, and he braced himself for an onslaught. It didn't come. Instead, she pivoted away from him suddenly, reached for a flashlight on the bureau and stalked out of the room. Dillon followed at her heels.

Murph had no choice. He had to go with her. "Sable, are you willing to shoot someone, to take a life? Do you even remember how to use the gun?"

"It's been a while, but I know how." Her footsteps didn't falter as she led the way down to the other end of the hallway, past the staircase, and opened the door to a walk-in closet. "This is where Grandpa stored his hunting gear."

The heavy smell of gun oil mingled with rancid doe scent that hunters used to attract bucks during hunting season. Sable didn't even pause to catch her breath. "I hated hunting season." She opened the lid of a long, metal gun chest and pulled out a black .22 pistol. It fit perfectly in her hands.

"You did say you knew how to use that," Murph said.

"Would you quit worrying? It's simple. Let's see…there are some bullets here somewhere." She searched all the junk in the chest, which was filled with gun cloths, hunting caps, everything but bullets. Cleaning wires and three half-used cans of gun oil tumbled onto the floor. Beneath it all lay a cardboard box. She opened the lid, and the flashlight beam fell on shotgun shells—and cubed chunks of silvery ore.

Murph heard her swift intake of breath. "Galena," she whispered.

Murph picked up a broken shotgun shell. Galena spilled from it.

"No." The beam of Sable's flashlight faltered.

Murph replaced the shell, and reached out to hold the flashlight steady. "Sable, I've already warned you not to jump to conclusions." He laid a hand on her shoulder.

She shrugged him away and slumped against the wall, squeezing her eyes shut. "Oh, Grandpa, how could you?"

"Sable."

"Don't say anything right now." She reached over to a glass gun case and swung the door open. The case was empty except for one short-barrel shotgun. She pulled it out. "He salted the mine. What else could it have been? He used this gun to shoot the ore into the soft sides of the Seitz mine."

"You can't be sure."

"See that reloader over there in the corner? He used it to fill these shells with ore, then he—" her voice caught "—he salted a barren hole in the ground."

Murph took her arm. "What are the gun and reloader doing here if he used it in Oklahoma?"

"He brought it back here. He certainly wouldn't want to leave evidence lying around Freemont."

"I'm sorry, Sable. I know you feel awful. I know how I would feel if—"

"Do you?" She shoved the shotgun back onto a shelf, kept the .22 pistol and closed the door. "Did you ever have to live with the humiliation of knowing a close family member cheated people out of their money?" Tears sparkled from her eyes in the dim light. She slumped onto a rickety chair.

He knelt beside her and took her hands in his. "Wait. We don't know all the facts—"

A faint, panicked female voice reached them suddenly from somewhere outside. "Help! Somebody come quickly! There's been an accident!"

SEVENTEEN

Murph and Sable rushed down the stairs to find Jerri and Bryce scrambling into the hallway from the family room. Perry burst through the kitchen door, his shirttail half out of his slacks, wiping his hands on a dish towel.

"What happened?" he cried. "Was that Audry? She was screaming like a banshee. I nearly caught the kitchen on fire."

"Someone hurt?" Jerri said. "Again?"

Murph shoved on his shoes. He was tying his laces when the back door flew open and Audry stumbled inside. She wore a hunter-orange knit cap and her thick, green wool coat.

"I found Simmons in the creek," she said breathlessly. "I've tried to get him up, but he's too heavy. The guy's freezing to a chunk of ice. Come and help me get him inside."

"Is he breathing?" Murph asked as he followed her out ahead of the others.

"He was when I first grabbed him, because he fought me. I had to wrangle him out of the creek, and he passed out on me."

Murph caught up with Audry halfway across the backyard.

"Look." She pointed toward the creek a couple hundred feet away. "I saw him from the kitchen window. When I got there all I could do was grab him by the sleeve and drag him to the bank. It's impossible to get any traction on that ice. I can't imagine what he was doing out there, the silly thing."

Murph recognized the muscular, broad-shouldered form of Simmons lying faceup, half out of the frigid, rushing water.

He scrambled over the treacherous ice to the man's side, sank to his knees and grabbed him by the shoulders. "Simmons!" he shouted, shaking him vigorously.

No response. He didn't appear to be breathing. Murph leaned close and felt no warmth of exhalation, heard no sound. He gently tipped the man's head back and lifted his chin to establish an airway.

Still no breath, no movement.

"What's going on?" Audry demanded behind him.

"He isn't breathing." Still holding Simmons's face tilted slightly upward, Murph managed to pinch the nostrils shut. He covered the man's mouth with his own and exhaled twice, deeply, slowly.

No response.

Murph slid the first two fingers of his right hand down into the hollow of the victim's neck, feeling for the carotid pulse. Simmons's pulse was weak.

"I've got to start CPR," he told Audry. "Get Sable—"

"I'm here," came her welcome voice behind him.

"Take his head, I'll do compressions." He scooted aside, unzipping Simmons's jacket while Sable slid into position at the man's head.

Murph was on his knees beside Simmons, in position to begin the first compression, when he saw Sable give another rescue breath.

With the fingers of both hands locked together over the lower third of Simmons's breastbone, Murph gave five compressions.

Sable was just leaning forward to breathe Simmons again when the man choked, gasped, sat up suddenly and coughed violently, spewing creek water in the chill air.

Murph held him steady until he stopped coughing.

Simmons jerked around, eyes wild, shivering.

"It's okay," Murph said. "We've got to get you inside. Let us help you up—"

"No!" Simmons cried. He choked again, a loud, rasping sound that brought up more of the creek water.

"Mr. Simmons," Sable said, leaning on Murph's shoulders to lever herself up to her feet, "you fell into freezing water. We've got to get you inside and warm you up. Can you walk?"

Simmons crabbed sideways in the water, his legs pumping ineffectively. "Can't feel them…can't feel my feet!"

Murph nodded to Sable, and together they helped the man up. "Hang on," he said, grasping Simmons around the waist and lifting him over his shoulder.

The drenching chill of water soaked through his shirt. Immediately, his feet slipped and he stumbled forward. "I need help. Is Craig—"

"I'm here." Bryce scrambled down to them. "Let me help."

Bryce, Murph and Sable manhandled Simmons's freezing body up the treacherous ice to the house, where Audry, Perry and Jerri waited.

Simmons choked again.

"Is he okay?" Jerri asked.

"What was he doing all the way down there, anyway?" Perry held the door open for them. "The outdoor privy is up here on the hill. Did he fall into the creek?"

"Of course he fell into the creek," Audry snapped. "What does it look like? He went swimming?"

Murph carried Simmons into the house and lowered him onto the hearth in front of the fire.

Sable rushed to take the wet clothes Murph peeled from Simmons's near-frozen body. "Perry, would you pump a pot of water and start it boiling?" she asked. "We'll need as much warm water as we can get. Bryce, he'll need something warm to drink. Audry—"

"Right, warm blankets." The lady ran up the stairs.

"We need to warm the blanket here on the grate. Craig, would you—" Sable turned, blinked. "Where's Craig?"

"I'll stoke the fire," Jerri said. "Craig's probably out still hauling wood." She disappeared down the basement steps.

Murph rubbed Simmons's hands. "Relax. We'll get you warm."

The man's teeth chattered. "I couldn't get out, nobody'd help me out of the water! You were all gonna stand there—" He coughed again, gasped for air, shook his head. He peered around the room, then back at Murph. "You'd've let me drown."

"You didn't drown, obviously." Murph eased Simmons backward and removed his footwear. His feet looked pale and were icy cold to the touch. "You're safe now. What happened?"

Still in her stocking cap and coat, Audry brought an armload of blankets. "Wrap one of these around him."

Simmons swore. "Keep her away from me!"

"Nonsense, you're delirious." Audry spread out another blanket.

"Get away!"

Audry frowned. "What's going on here?"

"You wouldn't let me out of that creek."

"I'm the one who dragged you out of there, you dolt!" she snapped. "You fell in and couldn't climb out on the slick ice, so don't blame me for your clumsiness. What were you doing out there, anyway?"

He raised a trembling hand and pointed at the knit cap on Audry's head. "You pushed me back in."

Perry came in carrying a mug from the kitchen. "Out of the way. I've got a warm cup of soup broth here. Come on, Simmons, drink up. This will warm you faster than—"

There was a thump from the front porch, and Dillon barked. The front door flew open, and Craig entered noisily, stomping his feet on the mat, unzipping the front of the coveralls he wore. His movements gradually slowed, as if he realized he'd become the center of attention.

"Where'd you get those clothes?" Audry demanded.

Craig pulled off his orange-red stocking cap and shrugged out of the dark green coveralls. "From the mudroom. Sorry I didn't mention it earlier, but there are a couple more coveralls and caps out there, in case anyone wants to go for a walk. Not that I'd recommend it." He tossed the outerwear over the hearth, then looked at the silent group with a frown. "What happened? What's wrong with Simmons?"

"Someone tried to drown me," Simmons snapped. "Someone in an orange cap and green coat."

"Well, it wasn't me," Audry scoffed. "What I want to know is what you were doing down at the creek." She pulled the knit cap from her head, and her short, gray hair bristled with static electricity.

"I wanted to see if there was a way out of here." Simmons shivered. "I checked the bridge, then started back to the house when I…lost my footing." Simmons jerked the blanket more tightly around his thick shoulders. "Then one of you pushed me under and wouldn't let me up."

Craig's dark brows lowered. "What's going on here? This is too much. There've been too many—"

"Later." Sable slipped past Murph. "I need to get my medical bag and check our patient."

After dinner, Sable left Murph and Craig sitting with Simmons by the fire while she escorted Bryce, Perry, Audry and Jerri up to the attic to see if they could find more clothes. The sky had continued to thicken with clouds as the sun went down, and the temperature hovered in the midtwenties. They were making plans for a longer imprisonment.

"I still think Simmons was hallucinating," Audry muttered as she searched through a huge old cedar chest in the light from Sable's powerful battery lantern. "Did you see how fast he recovered during dinner?"

"Yeah." Jerri lifted an old sweater and held it to the light. "But he wasn't as gruff. I think I like his postaccident personality. Maybe someone should've dunked him sooner."

Audry pulled out a blue suit that Sable remembered Grandpa wearing to special functions when she was a little girl. "I remember this," the older woman said.

"You do?" Sable asked.

Audry didn't meet her gaze. "I mean this style. It's back in fashion now, did you know? Too bad all the rest of us old things can't be back in fashion."

Jerri laughed from across the room. "I think you have to be dead first."

"Audry doesn't plan to die for a long, long time," Perry said. "She can't boss people from the grave."

"I've been good for you, admit it," Audry said. "We've probably run half a pound off you today. I heard the way you were panting when you carried water upstairs this afternoon."

"You'd pant, too, if you'd been up and down those stairs as often as I have today," Perry retorted.

Audry turned and appraised the rest of the attic. "Beautiful. This is almost like an antique store." She closed the lid of the chest and stepped around a box to get a closer look at an old pitcher and bowl set. "I love to look at old things and imagine the people who used them and the lives they led. This place is wonderful, and it's so huge."

Sable itched to ask Audry if Josiah Kessinger had ever been a part of her imaginings.

"Audry, look," Jerri said. "We could decorate a whole house with these things." She skirted more pieces of antique furniture and rows of labeled boxes. "Well, maybe a small cabin. Is that what you did, Sable? Audry, your room is furnished with antiques, isn't it?"

"Yes, I think most of them are family heirlooms." Audry picked up a ruby vase and held it to the light.

"Did Craig give you the grand tour?" Sable asked.

"No, and I wish he had," Audry said. "Jerri and I took our own tour while the others were preparing for sleep. Simmons complained about the noise we were making. Properly chastised, we went to bed."

"Leave it to Simmons," Perry remarked from the far corner of the attic, where he leaned against an old chest, examining a stack of pictures. "He seems to enjoy ruining a good time."

"That's okay," Jerri said. "Because the lights went out soon after, and I wouldn't't've wanted to be up here then." Jerri swept through a curtain of cobwebs and peered at an antique pie safe in the corner. "Bad luck seems to follow me lately. I wasn't supposed to be driving this route. I drove up from Oklahoma City and got stuck in Joplin because my replacement was stuck somewhere on a road in Kansas. I shouldn't be here."

Allowing the conversation to go on without her, Sable examined a pile of boxes along the back wall. "There's clothing over here. Why don't you three go through some of it while I show Bryce some of my brothers' old clothes." She hoped they would take the polite hint. She had brought them up here to find clothing, not antiques. She didn't want them rummaging around in any of the unopened boxes before she had a chance to search.

The attention of the others finally focused on the clothing, and she was free to concentrate on Bryce.

Many of Randy's old jeans looked as if they would fit the fifteen-year-old, so he stepped behind a huge wooden wardrobe to try them on. While Sable waited, she gazed around the attic. With studied nonchalance, she strolled over to a cardboard file box, but was disappointed to find that all it contained were pictures.

She sorted through them idly. Despite all the photographs she had taken over the years, her favorite rendition of the cave was a hand-drawn map Grandpa had been working on for years. He'd kept it as complete as possible, including every cavern and passage, almost every formation.

She walked over to the map, which hung on the wall between two windows. Once upon a time it had held a place of honor in the family room downstairs, but during the redecoration last year, Mom had insisted on taking it down. Ordinarily, when the power was on, an overhead spotlight could illuminate the map like a museum exhibit, but now in the half-light offered by the oil lamps, Grandpa's intricate drawing looked like hen scratchings on the wall.

She leaned closer to the map. A smudge of red ink caught her attention at the far right, near the end of a small passage. She held her light closer. The new drawing was in the shape of a funnel, and below it was a circle with markings…it looked like the face of a clock.

Her hand went up to the watch hanging from the silver chain around her neck.

Bryce came over wearing a pair of jeans Randy had outgrown many years ago. "These'll work."

Sable lowered her light and inspected the fit. They were a little loose on him, but serviceable. "Are there any other pairs? You may be here awhile."

"There's a couple more, and…hey, is that a map of the cave?" Bryce stepped closer and peered at the wall. "Wow! That's great."

"My Grandpa drew it, and he kept it updated as we explored and found more passages." As she spoke, she continued to search for pieces of the puzzle. The funnel…what could that be?

"Can we go down there?" Bryce turned to Sable beseechingly.

Sable didn't respond. A sinkhole? Could the funnel be a sinkhole?

"Maybe after we eat…or whenever you're free," Bryce was saying.

"Craig makes a good guide," Sable said, still distracted.

"But it was your grandpa who owned the cave, right? And he's almost like a legend, hearing Craig talk about him. Come on, Sable." Bryce leaned forward and gave her a dimpled, entreating smile. "Why can't you take me?"

She grinned. She could imagine him charming his mother with that smile. "We'll see."

"All right! When do we go?"

"I'd like to wait until morning."

He glanced toward the pictures Sable held in her hand. "Are those of the cave?"

She held them up in the glow of the lantern for him to see more clearly. "Yes, I took them myself. So, do those other jeans fit?"

"They're okay. I thought Craig said something about a collapse in the cave."

"A minor one, and nowhere near where we'd be going." Sable

set the old pictures back in the box, thinking about the sinkhole Grandpa had stepped into last November. "There's usually no danger of a collapse in a natural cave."

As Bryce joined Jerri and Audry and chattered to them about caves, Sable wandered to the far corner of the attic, where the door of Grandpa's safe was still camouflaged by a rack of clothing. Beside it was an old metal file box. Sable opened the rusted latch and pulled the lid back. There was a manila envelope at the top. On it was the return address of Tri-County Labs in Freemont, the same firm that had analyzed the silver inside the watch casing. She placed the tray into a box of clothing and covered it with an old blouse.

She had some work to do.

EIGHTEEN

The attic door squeaked softly when Sable pulled it shut behind her. She made sure the latch caught before turning away and picking up her box from the floor.

Jerri's voice drifted along the hall. "Probably can't fit into any of these, but I'll give it a try. Too bad Sable didn't have any fat family members."

"Perry's the one who needs to worry," Audry said.

"I heard that!" came Perry's voice from behind the closed door of the sewing room.

Sable carried the box to her room and closed the door behind her, then took the blouse from atop the metal tray. She raised the lid and pulled out the manila envelope. Inside, she found several stapled pages under a cover letter to Grandpa listing the enclosed three analysis reports. The next page was a smaller thin sheet of paper that reported on the galena, with a high content of lead.

Could that explain why the specimen collection downstairs had been rearranged? Maybe Grandpa had taken the galena and sphalerite to Tri-County Labs to be analyzed.

She turned the page to the analysis of the sphalerite. It was rich with zinc, but so what? Why even bother to have it analyzed? Grandpa knew it wasn't native ore. Or maybe he'd requested the analysis for another reason. Perhaps it was connected to the ore-filled shotgun shells in the gun closet? But how?

She flipped back to the cover letter. It specifically listed three analysis reports.

She knew where the third one was. She fingered the watch. Grandpa was up to something. But what did it all mean? What did it all have to do with Grandpa's death? And Noah's?

She slid the sheets back into their envelope and searched the rest of the tray. She found a couple of letters from Grandpa, which she opened and scanned.

It was correspondence written in November, when Grandpa had fallen into a sinkhole down by the creek and broken his ankle. In one letter, he thanked Mom for caring for him while he was incapacitated, then went on about what a good thing it was he fell. He'd found another opening to the cave, a sinkhole which was ordinarily underwater.

That was it—the fresh markings on the map upstairs. The funnel shape was a sinkhole. He'd already drawn it in.

In the second letter, he wrote about buying the Seitz property, in partnership with Noah and Otis. He didn't sound enthusiastic about the arrangement—an unusual attitude for Grandpa. Ordinarily, if he didn't feel passionate about something, he regarded it as a cue not to be involved.

But then, what made her think she knew all her grandfather's motives?

Nothing else in the letter seemed significant. She folded the pages, replaced them in the tray, and sifted through the remaining contents. Near the bottom she found an open envelope, again in Grandpa's handwriting, dated three days before Christmas. She quickly pulled out the pages.

I should never have signed my name to that contract, but now that I have, I'm as guilty as anyone else. I was so close I could have smelled the money—I thought this would be the best chance to get out of debt and get on top of things. What would it be like to be debt-free? Even better, we would never have to worry about mortgages or bill collectors again. Now I'm not sure. I need to talk to you and the kids about some things. Maybe even the police. There may still be a chance. I just want Sable out of this stinking town.

The police. Which police had he talked to?

She flipped the page, and gasped. There were copies of a note and a deed of trust. *To this place.*

Otis Boswell held the mortgage. At the top of the first page was a handwritten note in blue ink: "Just thought you'd appreciate a reminder."

The papers seemed to burn her fingertips, and the letter fell to the floor. Grandpa had borrowed the money from Boswell to buy the mine, using the house as collateral. Was that blue-inked note in Boswell's handwriting?

Sable slumped against the dresser. Boswell again. It always came back to him. What if he suddenly called in the loan? How deeply was he involved in this fraud? He always seemed to be lurking in the background.

Footsteps sounded gently along the hallway. There was a familiar creak, and then the footsteps receded in the direction from which they had come.

Sable shoved the metal tray beneath her bed. She wanted to slip back upstairs and get a better look at that map, to study the location of the funnel-sinkhole more closely.

For some reason, the huge old attic seemed darker than it had been earlier. And colder.

Hulking shapes of heavy furniture loomed around and over her, and inexplicably she developed an acute case of goose pimples. She raised her lantern high, dispelling a few of the shadows.

A small squeak echoed in the darkness. She paused to listen. A mouse, probably, but she shivered.

Jerri's laughter rang out from below, and Sable relaxed. She had never been afraid of mice before, no reason to start now.

The tall, mirrored bureau stood at the edge of the top step. She turned, caught the reflection of her movement in the mirror, and jumped.

"Stupid," she told herself impatiently. The fear in her eyes reflected back at her in the glow from her light. Did she appear this obviously spooked to the others?

Her safety and Murph's depended on how well she kept her fear in check, and how well she remained prepared for attack from any side.

Floorboards creaked beneath her feet as she stepped past the looming furniture, many pieces covered with sheets to protect them from dust.

She stopped between the dormer windows and looked at the boxes and chests stacked in rows. Something looked different. Of course, several of the smaller clothing boxes had been taken downstairs...but there was something else....

She inspected the rack of clothes in front of the safe. Had it been disturbed? She stepped closer and pushed the garments aside, holding the lantern high. The door was tightly closed, lock in place. But something...she glanced over her shoulder with a frown, and saw an empty spot between the two windows.

The map was missing.

But how could that be? She'd been the last one to walk out of here only a few minutes ago.

Feeling less and less comfortable, she went to the file cabinet. What else was missing? What if there had been someone up here besides Bryce, Audry, Perry and Jerri? There were hiding places...

"Stop being ridiculous," she whispered to herself. She needed to trust her own sense of hearing. She'd just left here a few minutes ago. Anyone would have had to pass her door. She would have heard footsteps.

So who took the map?

There was another rustle somewhere in the darkness—the skittering feet of a tiny mouse. Big deal.

But it sounded strangely like breathing. She held her own breath and froze, perfectly still. She did hear breathing.

Someone was in the attic with her. She studied the room again, her gaze roaming over sheet-covered furniture and boxes. She noted something different about the bulk of a tall pie safe covered by a paisley-print sheet. The sheet wasn't hanging right. The noises she'd heard earlier had come from that direction.

She crept quietly across the floor, the hairs at the back of her neck prickling. When she drew close enough to reach out and touch the sheet, a board squeaked beneath her foot.

The sheet moved with a jerk, lifted, came toward her and down over her head. She opened her mouth to cry out, and a rough hand shoved a wad of the sheet into her mouth. Her attacker jerked the material tightly around her body and shoved her to the floor. She whacked her elbow on the hardwood as she rolled over, kicking the air, struggling with the bonds as someone raced across the attic and down the steps.

She rolled the other way, kicked at the bottom of the sheet and gripped a loose end. By the time she was free of the sheet, it was too late to pursue her attacker.

NINETEEN

Murph tossed another log into the furnace in the basement and closed the heavy iron door. If the weather didn't break before long, he'd chop more wood, but not alone.

He touched the aching welt on his face, and he couldn't stop thinking about Sable's reaction when she thought he was badly injured or dead.

He smiled at the thought of her. Every time he looked at her, she was more beautiful than before, even with the darkness of grief and fear that had tightened the delicate features of her face over the past forty-eight hours. He wished he possessed the power—or at least the knowledge—to ease her pain.

"Lord, protect us," he whispered. "Strengthen my faith in You, because right now I'm really struggling with it. And let this draw Sable closer to You instead of damaging her fresh faith." He felt so helpless. As Uncle Noah used to say, it was especially good for a man to be forced to depend on the strength of Jesus Christ alone. That was where a man found his power…and his humility.

"Okay, so I need more humility, Lord," he murmured. Before he could continue in prayer, the sound of rushed steps reached him from above, and he looked up to find Sable racing down the basement stairs to him, holding her elbow. Her face was flushed, eyes wide.

"I was attacked in the attic."

"Attacked?" He rushed to her. "By whom? Are you hurt?"

"I didn't see who it was, and I'm not hurt, I just bumped my elbow."

"You went up there alone?" She exasperated him.

"It should have been safe. I could have sworn no one came past my door. You know how the stairs creak. I apparently surprised someone, and whoever it was hid. When I got too close, I was attacked."

"Thank God, literally, that whoever it was didn't see fit to do worse damage. Where's Dillon? Come upstairs with me." Murph took her hand. "Did you see anyone when you came through?"

"Most of the doors are closed—everyone is either trying on clothes or resting. Bryce is reading in the family room by candlelight."

Murph led the way cautiously up the steps to the living room. "Dillon," he called. "Here, boy."

They heard the click of canine nails on brick, and the German shepherd trotted out from the kitchen, ears perked forward, water dripping from his mouth. Even a watchdog had to eat and drink.

"Come, Dillon." Murph drew Sable up the stairs to the second floor. "I don't suppose you would agree to stay in your room with the door locked while I investigate."

"Nope."

Murph reached for the gun beneath his shirt as they crept along the hallway. "You could at least stay behind me."

To his surprise, she did as he suggested.

When they passed Audry's closed door, Murph heard feminine laughter. Jerri and Audry. That reduced the suspect list.

Maybe.

He felt the rush of cold air when he opened the attic door. He went up the steps into the huge, cavernous room, gun at the ready.

The attic was deserted. Dillon sniffed at the colorful sheet that had been tossed in a heap.

"Somebody must have sneaked past my bedroom door," Sable said. "Whoever it was hid under this sheet, then threw it over my head and wrapped me in it, knocked me down and ran."

Murph checked the shadows thoroughly with his flashlight. He found nothing.

He returned to Sable's side and reached for her, needing contact with her, to reassure her and himself that they were still okay. She stepped into his embrace and rested her forehead against his chest. He found himself wishing this were happening under different circumstances. And then he caught himself— no time to dream now.

"Did you get any sense of your attacker?" he asked. "Size? Was anything said?"

"Nothing. I was too startled."

He released her with reluctance, examined the welt on her elbow. "Please tell me you didn't try to give chase."

"By the time I got untangled, I was alone."

"Sable, you could have—"

"I know, I could have been killed."

Murph groaned, feeling more helpless every moment.

"You could have been, yes," he said at last. "You weren't. Thank God."

She looked up at him. "Speaking of God, if we belong to Him, why is this happening to us? Why aren't we being protected?"

"What makes you think we aren't? Look at all that's happened, and we're still here."

"But for how long?" she whispered. "Someone's stalking us for information." She drew back and looked into his eyes. "I might have just found a big clue."

"What kind of clue?"

"A deed of trust to this place, with Boswell's name on it."

"How? Why would he—"

"Grandpa apparently borrowed money against this place when he and Noah and Boswell purchased the Seitz mine. There was also a letter attached to two analysis reports, one for galena and one for sphalerite. The letter mentioned three. The third must have been for the silver. I'm not sure why Grandpa would have had those samples analyzed."

"Unless he suspected the ores really were native to the mine."

Sable turned away. "Or unless Grandpa planned to use them to dupe—"

"Don't say it. Stop allowing your disappointment with Josiah to cloud your deductive reasoning. He was human and he made mistakes, but I can't help feeling there are pieces to this puzzle that haven't been revealed yet."

She was silent for a moment, then nodded. "I thought I *could* depend on my knowledge of my grandfather, and I was apparently wrong."

"Don't jump to conclusions. We need to keep collecting pieces. I wonder if Boswell knows the results of the analyses."

"I believe he had his ways of finding out. For all I know, Grandpa had the ore analyzed just for that reason, so Boswell would think this place was worth more than it is, and would loan the required amount of money." Her voice wobbled. "And I'm not jumping to conclusions now, I'm just trying to make the pieces fit."

"But your grandfather didn't admit to that, did he? It seems to me, if he confessed one transgression, he would confess everything."

She stepped to a dormer window and looked out. "What if Otis Boswell knew about the silver assay? He's been after my grandfather to sell this place to him for a long time. He might have been willing to do anything to get it. Now he could call in the loan, and my family can't pay it. Otis Boswell could have controlled Grandpa, holding that mortgage over his head." She glanced over her shoulder at Murph. "The mortgage contract had a note attached to it that seemed like a taunt. And it wasn't in Grandpa's writing."

"A taunt?"

"I'm not trying to excuse Grandpa for what he did, but isn't it possible Boswell coerced him into it?" Sable asked.

"It's possible, if Josiah even did anything wrong in the first place." He joined her at the window. "Tell me, how many accident victims from the mines have you seen since you went to work at the clinic?"

She shrugged. "A few. The other docs are likely to see more, since they have more patients. I tend to see miners' wives and children. Why do you ask?"

"Because one reason Noah suggested I go to work at the clinic in Freemont was because he thought there might be some safety issues in the mines."

"Safety issues?"

"He thought Boswell cut corners to save money. It has seemed to me that the clinic received more mine accident victims than I would have expected in the six weeks I've worked there."

"I've seen some results of stupid actions," Sable told him, "but I always reported them properly. I'm sure the other docs are diligent about that, too."

"Of course you would do the right thing," he said.

Sable looked up at him, her gaze flitting across his features searchingly.

Murph was struck by the sensuality a woman could bring to a single glance. "Are you going to look for anything more tonight?" he asked. "Because if you are, I'm sticking to you like Dermabond adhesive."

"I'd like to try to make some sense out of what we already have." She spread her hands in a gesture of frustration. "My grandfather placed himself in deep debt putting his three grandchildren through college. We were all paying him back, but if I'd known he was struggling, I'd have applied for a school loan and never allowed him to pay for my education."

"Maybe he didn't want you to try to talk him out of doing what he wanted to do."

"We're missing something," she said, looking at him.

"It looks like we're missing a lot. If you insist on going down into the cave in the morning, I'm going with you."

"Bryce will be with me. I want to check a hunch."

"Is it important?"

"It could be," she said. "I'd like to see the crystal cavern again, and I want to look for a sinkhole my grandfather mentioned. The map had some new markings on it, and I think it had the outline of a clock face."

"A clock?"

"Or a watch." She touched the pocket watch. "Our intruder took the map, and I'm not sure about the location."

"Then we'll look for it together. I want you safe."

"You just want to go spelunking."

"You have a problem with that? Sable, your strength and independence are admirable. In fact, they are two of the many qualities that attract me to you." He lowered his head and kissed her quickly, before she could stop him—before he could stop himself. The touch of her soft lips on his was almost his undoing. "But in this case self-sufficiency is just plain dangerous," he said, trying to keep his voice under control. "Accept help where you can get it. We don't know who else we can trust."

He saw the sudden vulnerability in her eyes and he almost regretted what he had just done, kissing her like some impetuous teenager. But then, in the fleeting expressions that washed across her face, he saw something else—something he knew she would not want him to see. He saw desire flash in her eyes. He couldn't stop the grin that spread across his face.

Sable pulled from his grasp and spun away without a word. He watched her bulldoze past a stack of boxes, a dresser, a washstand. He followed meekly behind her. Time to play it cool for a while.

This time, Sable couldn't hear the squeak of the attic floor over the roaring in her ears as she rushed across the darkened room. She was no longer afraid of the shadows.

Instinctively, she raised a hand to her lips, acutely aware of Paul Murphy's nearness, and desperate to concentrate on the danger—and the puzzle—at hand. It was difficult.

Murph picked up the sheet, shook it out, searched around the edges of the pie safe. "You've told me about some of the records you found up here. Where is the confession note?"

Sable reached into the front pocket of her slacks. "I've kept it on me." She spread it open in the glow from Murph's flashlight. Together, they began to read it again.

Sable caught something significant quickly. She looked up at Murph, struggling to temper her sudden surge of hope. "I don't think this is a confession at all."

"What do you mean?"

She pointed to the first paragraph. "He says it's been more than eleven years since Grandma died. Grandma died twenty years ago. That's a lot more than eleven. I was so stunned by the confession that this didn't register before."

"What could it mean?"

"I'm not sure," she said. "The first sentence hints for us to look closely at the words he uses." She pointed to the second paragraph. "He says here that by the time we get this letter, we will have already heard the story. Murph, he only used that term when he was telling a tall tale. He would trick us that way, tell us a long, fun story about his past, have us believing him, then explain that it was just a story. Fiction."

"But why write the note at all?" Murph asked. "Why not just talk to you in person?"

"It seems he would only do that if he thought he wouldn't be able to talk to us," she said.

"Keep reading. What else do you see?"

She continued scanning. "Here it says he's sorry to miss my birthday party this year because he knows how much I love them. He knew I hated birthday parties."

"So why mention your birthday? And why use the number eleven when it should have been twenty? He also mentions the watch being a combination Christmas-birthday—"

"Combination!" Sable exclaimed.

"And look—it says, 'Don't worry, I'm *safe* in the afterlife.'"

Sable slid the note back into her pocket as she led Murph through the shadows to the far wall. She shoved the clothing rack aside to reveal the dark gray mass of the old safe.

"Does anybody besides family know about this old safe?" Murph asked.

"I don't think so, except maybe Craig."

Murph raised his flashlight to illuminate the numbers on the dial. "We have the number eleven and your birthdate. Let me see the note again."

She pulled it out of her pocket once more and spread it in the light. "Try turning it clockwise to eleven." She held the paper out for him. "See the word *forgive?* That could mean forward. Then turn it back, counterclockwise to two, because he uses the word *back*. Then clockwise to one, counter to five."

"Got it."

"Did it click?"

"No." He tried again, adding her birth year. "Nothing."

There was a squeak of floorboards on the attic stairs. "Sable? You up here?" Audry called. "It's Jerri and me. Think we could look for more clothes? Jerri needs—"

"I need fat lady clothes." Jerri chuckled.

Murph shoved the clothing back into place while Sable stuffed the note into her pocket. So much for further sleuthing tonight. She was disappointed, yet at the same time vastly relieved.

Fiction. It was all fiction. Maybe Grandpa isn't guilty, after all.

Soon it would be time for bed, and first thing in the morning they'd be searching the cave for more clues.

TWENTY

Sable scrambled over a ledge of limestone and straightened inside the cave. She aimed her light along the passage, and to the mouth of the rocky pit that she and her brothers had always been warned to avoid. It was the most dangerous place in the whole cavern system.

She stepped forward so the others could come through, and as she waited, she reacquainted herself with the dark cavern. It was a homecoming. She had many good memories here, when she and Peter and Randy—and many times Craig and his sister, Candace—had explored and shared the wonders of this special playground.

Bryce joined her in the dripping silence. Murph and Craig followed, walking single file into the deep, hovering darkness.

Murph played the beam of his flashlight over every inch of the cave. The light played on a cluster of quartz crystals, then moved back to the pit.

When the group climbed down to the next cavern, Bryce stopped and gazed in awe at a room of rust-colored formations. "This is great." He reached out to touch a tall column, glistening with moisture. "Oops." He jerked his hand back. "I almost forgot. I learned in science class that you aren't supposed to disturb a living cave. Even our walking here changes its growing patterns just a little." He gestured around, at the multitude of stalactites and rising stalagmites colored by iron deposits.

"You're right about a cave being a living environment," Sable told him. "This is a world all its own. It even breathes with the rise and fall of the barometer; that's why the air is so fresh, instead of musty as you might expect." She stepped over to a cranny where a whirlpool once flowed. "This is where my brother, Peter, tried to skin-dive and nearly drowned."

Craig laughed. "I remember that. He almost drowned me when I tried to get him out."

"Serves you right," Sable said. "You helped him and Randy play tricks on me all the time. Remember when Randy dressed up in that sheet like a ghost, and jumped out in front of me down at the end of the soda straw passage?"

"I remember he dropped his flashlight and broke it."

"What happened then?" Bryce asked.

Sable grinned at Craig. "I turned off my flashlight and found my way home in the dark."

"And just left him down here," Craig said. "He got lost, and Sable got into big trouble, especially when she told her Grandpa she wasn't sorry."

"The boys had been picking on me all summer," Sable said.

Craig laughed. "You were spoiled, admit it."

"Grandpa appreciated my honesty."

"The rest of us would've had our hides tanned. When you complained about the way we picked on you, he gave you lessons in street fighting."

"I never misused that knowledge," Sable said.

Murph turned to her with a grin. "Oh, really?"

Sable smiled back. "That's right, I only use it when pestered, provoked or detained in a dangerous situation."

"Happens to you a lot, huh?" Craig said.

Sable and Murph shared a quick look of understanding.

"Something good came of that incident," Sable told Bryce. "The search for my brother led to the discovery of another passage. Grandpa was ecstatic. He was always interested in finding new passages and intriguing formations." *And sinkholes. And...silver?*

She wished she had that map—and that she'd paid more attention to the new markings on it. Unfortunately, it might now be leading someone else to a new discovery. If he or she knew what to look for.

But how could that be? Only she and Murph were aware of the contents of her watch case.

The group entered the next cavern, where the limestone ceiling had buckled, revealing a gaping blackness above it.

"A breakdown cavern," Bryce said. "Cool."

Sable stepped over a boulder and passed a raised ledge where she and her brothers had often hidden from one another.

The passage split, and a dry streambed angled downhill from the familiar limestone path.

Craig stopped, shining his light along the descending rocky bed into the darkness beneath a low ledge. "Hey, this looks like a new passage." His baritone voice quickened with excitement. He turned to Sable. "Why don't you let me check it out. May not go anywhere, and if it doesn't I'll catch up with the rest of you."

"You'd miss a trip to the crystal cavern just to crawl on your stomach over a bunch of rocks?" she teased.

"Radical idea, I know." He grinned at her.

Craig and her brothers had always competed with her, and with each other, trying to be the first to explore a new passage, or to scale a challenging wall.

"It could dead-end ten feet down," she said. "If it goes anywhere, maybe you can show us later."

"Let me go with you, Craig," Bryce said with youthful exuberance. "Please?"

"If we're late for lunch," Sable said, "Audry will—"

"I'm just going to check it out, Sable," Craig said. "I'll catch up with the rest of you."

"And me. I'm going with Craig," Bryce said.

"You may have to do a lot of crawling and scooting on the ground," Sable warned Bryce. "You could get filthy."

"I'll wash these clothes myself when I get back to the house, okay?" Bryce pleaded.

"Sounds fine with me," Craig said. "We can let Sable and Murph go on ahead, then we'll catch up when we can. If it gets too late—let's say, after eleven—we'll head back toward the house. Sable, what time do you have?" He gestured to the pocket watch that hung around her neck.

"This doesn't keep time. Murph, what—"

"What do you mean it doesn't keep time? That thing's always kept good time." Craig raised his flashlight to peer at the antique.

"Take my word for it, Craig," she said drily.

He shrugged. "Anyway, I'm going to check out this passage."

She noticed Murph peering back the way they had come, the beam of his light poking into the shadows.

Craig followed Murph's gaze. "Are you worried we've gotten lost?"

Murph inspected three more dark corners, then shrugged. "No, I thought I heard something. I'm just a little edgy." He glanced at Sable. "Simmons got up when I did this morning. I haven't seen him since."

"He was in the family room earlier," Bryce said. "He and I played a game of checkers."

"Was he still there when we came down here?"

"Nope, he left when I went to put my shoes on."

"I'm heading down," Craig called over his shoulder as he dropped to his knees and crawled beneath the rocky ledge.

Bryce followed him.

Sable watched them disappear into the narrow tunnel, listening to Bryce's eager questions and Craig's good-natured replies. Like a couple of kids. Craig was a grown man who could take care of himself. He would extend that care to Bryce.

"So tell me where we're going," Murph said.

She aimed the beam of her light down the passage to their right. "This path wanders back for about a half mile before it reaches the white room and the crystal cavern."

"The place Audry mentioned to Bryce."

"Right."

"And you're wondering why," Murph guessed.

"You bet I am." As Sable led the way, Murph took slow, thoughtful steps, studying every shadow with deep concentration.

After about fifteen minutes of walking at a turtlelike pace, Sable glared at Murph over her shoulder. "Murph, are you sure you want to go on? You don't seem—"

"Come here and look at this." He aimed his light on the clay trail. "Footprints."

"You heard us talk about all the times we came down here."

"But look where they lead." He followed them with the light around a rust-colored column and back out to the trail. "I know this sounds strange, but I think they're fresh."

"How can you tell?"

Murph inhaled. "Take a whiff. Smell anything that doesn't belong in a cave?"

Sable sniffed the air, watching Murph quizzically.

"Cologne," Murph said. "Simmons uses it instead of bathing. It reeks."

"You already know Simmons was down here, you saw him here yesterday."

"The scent wouldn't linger that long."

"So maybe he came back down this morning," Sable said. "Do you think someone really tried to attack him yesterday?"

"No, I think he fell into the creek and his macho pride was hurt when a woman old enough to be his grandmother had to pull him out."

She stepped ahead of Murph. "Let's go check out the crystal cavern before Craig and Bryce catch up with us."

"That's the place that was salted back in the forties, right?" Murph asked.

"Yes."

"I'd like to see it."

Sable led the way through a long, narrow passage, the powerful glow of her light illuminating more formations, alien sights to most people, but familiar to her. There was no path here, but they traveled easily, except in a few places, where the clay was wet and sticky, or where they had to climb over a pile of rocks. Occasionally, the passage split, and Sable indicated the markers she used to find her way. At one intersection she showed Murph a whirlpool dome, and at another she pointed to a unique helectite formation.

The passage widened at last, and by habit, Sable hesitated before stepping into a broad cavern with a low ceiling and walls of uninterrupted paleness. This white room had always seemed like a near-sacred place to her. The beams from their flashlights reflected from the smoothly undulating surfaces with a super-natural incandescence.

Murph whistled softly. "No wonder you love this cave."

"This and the crystal cavern are my favorites." She aimed her light to the left. "The crystal cavern is in there. See that ledge of rock above it? It's a natural bridge, leading from nowhere to nowhere. I used to hide there and jump down in front of my brothers to frighten them."

Murph chuckled. "You gave as good as you got."

"You'd better believe it."

"You still do."

She grinned. "You don't know the half of it."

"I'm learning quickly."

The white flowstone passage opened into a larger cavern angling up to the right. Murph entered the huge, domed room. Sable was about to follow when a soft sound arrested her attention—like the scuffing of a shoe on stone.

As Murph disappeared from sight, she turned and listened. Had Craig and Bryce reached a dead end, and decided to join her and Murph, after all?

She stepped along a dry streambed and around a curve in the passageway, then down a graduated shelf of water-sculpted stone. She circled another pure white column, then stopped and gazed down into the dark cavern where water had once splashed and swirled wildly.

"Just as I thought," she said softly.

The cavern was almost dry. Stooping, she shone her light into the mysterious depths. Sphalerite and galena glittered, shattering the brilliance of Sable's light into thousands of pinpoints, illuminating the cavern with the glow of a beam through a prism.

She frowned. "Murph?"

"Yes?" he called from the white room.

"You might want to see this."

He rounded the corner quickly, his flashlight increasing the sparkle in the pit. "Did you find something?"

"Look at the ore. There wasn't this much the last time I was down here."

"How can you be sure? When was the last time you saw this place without water?"

"Two years ago. There wasn't this much ore." She pointed to a chunk of galena, about a quarter-inch wide. "Would you like to estimate about how long the water's been depositing limestone over that ore?"

Murph bent down to get a better view. "I don't see any limestone over it."

"None," she said. "I think this is recent. Within the past year—maybe even the past few months."

"Why would anyone salt this place?" Murph studied the ore, then turned and shone his light on the quartz crystal along the sides of the limestone bridge above them. "Any theories?"

"None." She studied the flicker of her light against a white protrusion at the bottom of the pit. The protrusion was just to the left of a stream of opaque, mineral-rich buttermilk water. She thought of the analysis sheets, and wondered where the analyzed ore had originated.

She lay on her stomach at the edge of a limestone ledge and shone her light over the gleaming surface. "High-grade silver would be black. Do you see anything that looks like it might be tarnished silver? Maybe a fine thread of black?"

Murph knelt next to her, and together they aimed their lights over the vertical sides of the cavern walls, methodically examining every sparkle, every mark, every indentation in the limestone.

Sable returned her examination to the bottom of the cavern,

where a set of matching indentations a few feet from the stream drew her attention. She aimed her beam directly on them, and frowned.

"Footprints," she said.

Murph peered over her shoulder. "Someone's been down here since it dried up."

"But Craig said he hadn't come this far."

"Can you trust his word?"

She frowned at the doubt in Murph's voice. "Of course."

"What about your brothers?"

"Peter and Randy both told me they'd been too busy to explore lately. Maybe Grandpa—"

"Look, someone's been digging down there, too." The ray of Murph's light showed freshly disturbed earth and rocks.

"Do you think—"

The sound of scattering pebbles echoed from the darkness behind them.

Murph swung around. "What was that?"

There was scuffling, and a movement of shadow from the natural bridge above and behind them. Rocks clattered down. Murph lunged forward to protect Sable from the rockslide, and something—someone—shoved them from behind.

Sable shifted to retain her balance, and the ledge beneath her right foot crumbled. Her arms flew out automatically, and she lost her grip on her flashlight. It bounced with a clatter against rock and earth and landed in the pit below.

"Murph!" She fell hard on the edge of the pit and clawed at the limestone floor, feeling herself slide.

Murph grabbed her shirt. "Sable!"

She reached up and grasped his arm, arresting her slide. Then the ledge crumbled completely, and she cried out as wet earth and loose rocks fell beneath her. She scrambled to get back onto solid ground, but the earth continued to fall away beneath her feet. Sharp rocks dug into her legs.

She felt something tug at her shirt in the darkness.

"Reach for me!" Murph said. "I've got—"

The ledge gave way, and her shirt ripped. Sable flung her free arm up to catch at Murph, but her blouse tore loose from his grip. She plunged down into the darkness, fighting the mud, until she landed, with a cry of pain, at the bottom.

TWENTY-ONE

Murph lay panting at the edge of the pit, his eyes straining against the impenetrable darkness. The distant echo of footsteps reached him; whoever had pushed them was running away, stumbling over rocks in flight.

"Sable, are you okay?" he shouted. "Sable, say something! Answer me!" Frantically, he felt around for his flashlight. "Sable!"

He heard a rustle of movement several yards below him, and a soft groan.

"Sable? Wake up!"

No answer.

He dug through the damp earth until he felt the end of his flashlight, and discovered that it hadn't gone out, it had only been caked with clay. When he wiped it off, the glow lit the cave once again, and he pointed it at Sable. Her pale, still face frightened him.

"Sable!" he shouted. "You've got to wake up, sweetheart! You've got to hear me!"

He searched for a rope, for handholds or footholds on the face of the cliff that had just collapsed with her. Nothing. He studied the length of the ledge and beyond, to the bare rock face of the wall that circled the cavernous pit and rose above the ledge on which he stood. He saw nothing but slick limestone and scattered fragments of galena.

The pit was at least fifteen feet deep; he couldn't climb into it and back out without a rope, and he couldn't risk both himself and Sable getting stuck down there. No doubt, someone would eventually come to find them, but what if Sable was badly injured? Murph might be forced to go for help. If only he could take her in his arms, hold her, make sure she was still breathing...

Craig and Bryce might not even come this way if they found the other passage more interesting. He couldn't just sit and wait. But he couldn't leave Sable.

"Sable? Please, can you hear me?"

He waited endless seconds as his flashlight illuminated her deathly still features, her hair slithering like a living thing in the tiny stream of milky water beside her head. "Lord, please!" He couldn't tear his fearful gaze from her face.

She moved.

"Sable, wake up!"

Her dark lashes fluttered, and she winced.

"Thank you, God!" he shouted. "Sable, look up at me!"

Sable's mind, foggy with pain, steadied at the sound of Murph's voice, concentrating hard on it, struggling against dizziness.

"Murph," she croaked, her head throbbing with the effort to form her words. "You okay?"

"Forget about me. Lie still until you've done an assessment. Did you hit your head on something?"

Sable squinted up toward the sound of his voice, and her blurred sight caught the ghostly shape of his head above the beam of his flashlight. "Murph?" Her voice sounded louder to her as the pounding in her head receded. "You sure you're okay? Did you see who hit us?"

"*See* him? I *felt* him."

"Was it a him?" Her voice drifted...

"We'll deal with that later. I heard someone run away. It's you I'm worried about. Where are you hurt? Can you move your hands and feet? Come on, Sable, stay with me. You need to assess your injuries."

Sable became aware of the scratches on her arms, of the pain at the back of her head, of the water swirling close to her ears. Tentatively, she moved her legs and hips, then sighed with relief. "I don't think anything's broken, except maybe my skull." Her head throbbed. She wiped something sticky from her face. "That's…that's not blood, is it?"

"Can you move without pain?"

She noticed he didn't reply directly to her question. "Blood, Murph. Is it blood?"

"I can't tell for sure, but from here it looks like mud. *Can you move without pain?*"

Sable groaned. "Have a heart. I can't even see with you shining that stupid light in my eyes." The brightness eased. "Thanks." She struggled to sit upright. A piercing stab of pain shot through her head when she moved. She slumped sideways into the sticky clay, momentarily comforted by the coolness against the side of her face.

"Where are you hurt?" Murph demanded.

"My head. I must've hit it on a rock in the water."

"Are you dizzy?"

Darkness converged on her again. The cave whirled around her, scattering the beams of Murph's flashlight.

"Sable, talk to me! Now!"

"Murph, I just can't seem to—"

"You've got to try to stay conscious. Concentrate. Are you dizzy?"

She lay still. "I think I'll be okay in a little while. I don't know where my flashlight fell. Can you shine yours around and find it?"

She closed her eyes as he swept his beam around. Pain washed over her.

"I'm sorry, sweetheart, but I can't find it."

"Go get Craig and Bryce."

"And leave you here alone? What if the attacker returns?"

"We need help now."

"I could come down and boost you out."

"I…uh…I don't think I can make it out. Please, Murph, get help." Sable felt around her and at last her fingers came into contact with a hard, oblong object in the water. "I've found the flashlight. Now will you please go?"

"Does it work?" Murph asked.

She grasped it more firmly and tried to pull it out of the water. It wouldn't budge. She moved her fingers farther down and jiggled, dug around the end of the object. How could it have become so imbedded? It finally loosened in her fingers, and she pulled it out. From the reflected glow of Murph's light against the crystals in the cave wall, she saw more than she wanted to see.

"It isn't…it's not the flashlight after all," she said. Tingles of shock fled through her, renewing the pounding pain in her head. Now she knew what the white protrusion was in the water, what had dented her head. A human long bone.

"Sable, you need to remain still until I get back with help. Will you do that?"

"Yes," she said, clamping down hard on her panic.

"That means you'll have to sit here in the dark until I come back."

"Yes," she said, her voice barely above a whisper. "Go now. Quickly. I learned a long time ago not to be afraid…afraid of the dark." But what was in the dark right now? Was the stalker still up there somewhere, waiting? Would Murph be in more danger on his own?

He stood. "I'll be back as soon as I can. Just stay calm."

"Do you remember how to get back?"

"I remember," he said softly. "You're a wonderful guide. You showed me every marker."

Sable heard him moving off, as if a great distance already separated them. Blackness covered her. She might die here. Or Murph might, if he wasn't careful. She couldn't stand the thought of that.

"Murph?"

He stopped. "Yes?" Gentle, so tender.

"Please be careful. Don't let anyone get you."

"Nobody's going to get me." She heard him turn to walk on.

"Murph?"

He stopped again.

"I mean it. I...couldn't handle it if something happened."

"I'll be careful. Stay awake, Sable. You can do it." He raced away, the echo of his footsteps fading as she lay with her eyes closed in the darkness.

The pain in her head slowly receded to a dull throb, but her head still whirled, and nausea clenched her stomach.

She had been in complete darkness like this lots of times. The good thing was if she couldn't see anyone, no one could see her, either. Murph had said he'd heard their attacker running away. It meant whoever it was feared being seen and maybe would not be coming back this way.

Shadows loomed huge as Murph raced from a narrow passageway into another shadowed cavern. He scrambled over a slippery rock, then frowned at the forked section of passages.

He rushed headlong down the right fork, and immediately encountered a filmy, white mist. It didn't thicken as he made his way. Had Craig and Bryce found a viable passage, or would he have to follow them through this labyrinth to the end to get help?

This cave was filled with tunnels, probably false passages. No wonder Sable's brother had gotten lost down here.

He ducked his head to go beneath a low rock and heard another sound over the splashing water—metal hitting rock.

He swung around, aiming his light back the way he had come. "Who's there?"

No answer.

"Craig? Bryce? Where are you?"

Still no answer. No sound of retreating footsteps. He backtracked, listening hard, but hearing no more.

* * *

Slowly, with great care, Sable splashed her face with water from the small stream that trickled past her. She could only pray that their attacker hadn't followed Murph.

Carefully, she shifted positions. Her head throbbed. But she could tell, even through the pain and nausea, that it was getting better. She'd taken falls before, although maybe not quite as painful as this one.

She splashed more water in her face, wondering about the human bone.

No one in the family had ever taken seriously the story about the previous owners finding silver here, because silver didn't occur naturally in this part of Missouri. If it was found at all, it was only as a by-product of another mineral—a valuable by-product.

But the two earlier owners who had disappeared—they might well have believed in the myth of hidden silver, and they might have prospected for it down here. Had she just landed on the remains of one of those partners? The men could have drowned in the flood that had swept through here at the time of their disappearance.

A new line of thought occurred to her: The ceiling collapse in the nearby cavern had happened within the past century—a rarity. Could there have been a small earthquake around the fault line? And if so, was it possible that the owners were in it at the time? This leg bone could have washed to this pit later, during another flood.

A distant sound reached her, a rattle of rocks. She caught her breath and struggled to sit up. Her eyes opened wide, peering into the darkness. Did she detect a shade of light? A movement of shadow? It could be Murph, returning with Bryce and Craig. Or it could be the attacker. Wouldn't Murph have called out to her by now?

Sable scrambled away from the streambed. She was about halfway between the ledge from which she'd fallen and the wall on the other side of the cave. Her right hand touched some pebbles, scattering them, sending them splashing into the water.

She heard a footfall, then another, but she saw no flash of light. None. How could someone be walking in the darkness?

The footsteps neared, softly. She stared into the blackness. Had she suffered some kind of blindness from her head injury?

Another footstep, directly above her. She stared hard into the darkness. Was that a very faint green glow? Like the eyes of an animal reflected in headlights, only not as bright.

Ghost eyes.

She blinked, rubbed her eyes and looked back up at the ledge. The glow dipped and disappeared.

She heard the clink of metal, and another scuffle of footsteps.

She scrambled backward in the mud, feeling for the bone she had thrust aside. If only she could keep her mind clear, maintain her bearings. She found the bone.

She crept backward, feeling for the limestone wall. There was a tiny crawl space about five feet to her right. She had explored it once, barely fitting through.

She heard a rustle of fabric and turned back toward the ledge, saw the ghost eyes bobbing in the darkness once again. She couldn't be hallucinating…could she? She skittered backward and struck her tailbone on a rock. With a muffled groan, she rolled onto her side and reached back for a rock. Still clutching the bone in her left hand, she drew herself onto her knees and flung the rock toward the ledge. It hit with a clatter and bounced back into the cavern.

The glow disappeared and she heard more sounds of scuffling, the scattering of tiny rocks and dirt. For the first time, she heard heavy breathing.

She bent down and felt for another rock, found one and threw it as hard as she could toward the last place she'd seen the glow.

The glow reappeared for a few seconds, as if the ghost had turned to get its bearings again before continuing down.

She scrambled toward the tiny passage.

* * *

Murph scuttled beneath the rocky ledge, picking his way with speedy care along the dry streambed. He recognized where he was now, at the passage that Craig and Bryce had taken.

"Craig?" he called. "Bryce!"

He had to drop to his hands and knees and crawl over a scattering of rocks for about twenty feet, and then suddenly the ceiling lifted and the passage broadened. Here he encountered more fog, thicker this time, so thick it reflected the beam of his flashlight back at him.

"Craig! Are you down here?"

He squeezed through another narrow, passage. "Craig!"

A distant voice echoed from the limestone wall, perhaps a hundred feet away. He scrambled up a steep incline, the fog so thick now he had to cup the beam of his flashlight with his hand to keep the glare from blinding him.

"Help! We need help!" He stepped out into another columned room, and stopped. "Sable fell! I need help getting her out."

"We're coming!" It was Craig.

Murph waited. Craig and Bryce emerged through the fog a few moments later, breathless and dirty.

"What happened?" Craig asked.

"Sable fell in the crystal cavern. We need help."

"Let's go!" Craig said, leading the way.

Sable threw another rock, and another. Her head throbbed with the exertion. Finding a break in the limestone wall, she crawled sideways into a protective tunnel.

There was a sound of shoes scraping against rock. She turned. The ghost eyes hovered only a couple of yards above her. Murph wasn't going to return in time.

She screamed. The ghost grabbed her by the throat. Her watch chain broke. She screamed again, falling into darkness.

A scream echoed through the cave. Murph pulled himself up from the low passage and raced toward the crystal cavern ahead of the others. "Sable!" Panic spurred him through the last two caverns, along the rocky passage and out the other side.

They reached the pit. Total blackness.

"Sable!" Murph shouted. He aimed his light around the darkened crevices of the pit until he saw her blue nylon jacket. She lay in the mud.

He handed his light to Bryce. "I'm going down."

"Wait," Craig said. "We need a rope."

"We don't have time to get a rope!" Murph said.

Craig took off his jacket. "We can use this. It's denim, it'll hold. Here, take one end. Can't have you falling, too."

Murph grabbed the sleeve and allowed Craig to lower him as far as possible, then jumped the last few feet. He rushed to Sable's side just as she raised her head and began to stir.

"Sable, what happened? Are you okay?"

She turned glazed eyes toward him. "Someone came after me," she whispered "They got my watch…couldn't see…ghost eyes."

She wasn't making sense. He checked her pupils. They were equal and reactive. "You can see me now, can't you?"

She peered up at him. "I can see fine."

He did a hasty neurological exam. Whatever had happened to her a few minutes ago, she was stable now.

"Let's get you out of here," he said.

With a sidelong glance at the water flowing lethargically past them a couple of feet away, she reached for Murph. "Maybe I was hallucinating. Or maybe we really do have a ghost," she mumbled as she leaned against him.

With help from Craig and Bryce, Murph hauled Sable up the side of the embankment. "Let's get her to the house."

As Murph lifted her into his arms, she leaned close to his ear. "Did you hear me? The ghost took my watch."

TWENTY-TWO

Murph carried Sable up the basement steps, and for the first time in her life, she was relieved to escape the cave. She felt outraged and violated, frustrated and desperate. She held on to Murph with all her strength.

When he carried her through the door into the living room, Audry looked up from the sofa and gasped.

"What on earth!" She tossed her crossword puzzle aside and jumped to her feet. "Sable! What happened?"

"I fell." She didn't have the energy to explain.

"Here, Murph, sit her down on the sofa. Craig, bring me some towels. We'll need to clean her off before we can see where she's hurt."

"Murph has already checked me for injuries," Sable said, relenting enough to allow Audry to help her remove her mud-caked nylon jacket. "I hit my head. It'll be okay." She hoped. "Ice, though. I could use some ice."

"I'll get some," Bryce said and ran into the kitchen.

Audry pulled off Sable's boots. "How did it happen?"

"I told you, I fell."

Audry rolled her eyes, taking the towels Craig brought. "Thanks, that'll be enough. Now, Sable, let's get you up to your room and get these filthy clothes off."

"First, tell me where everyone has been since we left."

Audry stopped bustling around Sable. "What do you mean? We've been right here, of course. Where did you expect us to go?

Boys, if you're hungry, there's some lunch in the kitchen. Jerri had KP, but you'll have to serve yourselves now."

"Where is she?" Sable asked.

"I think she might have gone upstairs to the attic."

"And Perry and Simmons?" Murph asked.

"I'm not concerned about those two right now, I'm concerned about Sable," Audrey said.

"Just tell us where they are," Sable said sharply, finding strength in her indignation.

Audry shook her head. "You people don't make any sense. I heard Dillon growling upstairs earlier and went up to find a face-off between him and Simmons in the hallway."

"When did this happen?" Murph asked.

"Oh, I'd say about twenty minutes ago. Couldn't tell you what it was about, but I let Simmons know right quick he'd better not be disturbing anybody's stuff. He's kept a low profile since. As long as he keeps the fire stoked, I'm happy."

"And Perry?" Sable asked.

"I saw him carrying water upstairs about thirty minutes ago. Now you men shoo on out of here. I'm getting Sable upstairs. Honey, can you walk?"

"Of course I can." Sable stood up. "Did you see either of the men before that? What have they been doing since we left?"

"Honey, I don't keep track of those two." Audry clicked her tongue and shook her head. "Simmons sure wasn't thrilled with your dog, though. Let's get you upstairs to bed."

"You're not really putting her to bed, are you?" Murph asked.

"I didn't say sleep, I said bed. I'll watch her."

"I'll help," Murph insisted.

"Not while I help her undress, you won't. Now give us some room to work, why don't you?"

"I don't need help undressing," Sable said.

"You don't need to be left alone, either."

Bryce returned with a plastic zipper bag filled with ice. Sable took it gratefully and held it against her skull.

Upstairs, Audry's hands were gentle as she washed away the

top layer of drying mud from Sable's face and arms. "I don't see any blood."

"Just mud," Sable said. The ice felt wonderful, but her head still throbbed. "Audry, how much did you see of the others while we were gone?" She hesitated. "And what did you do?"

Audry shuffled through the top drawer of Sable's dresser, selected a T-shirt, and tossed it to Sable. "I can't help wondering why you're concerned about this now, when your health is more important."

Sable changed quickly into the T-shirt. "If there were strangers in your home, wouldn't you want to know what they were doing with their time?"

Audry tucked the muddy blouse under her arm and searched through the dresser until she found an old pair of scrub pants. She handed them to Sable. "I think I was taking a bath before you left."

"I thought I heard water splashing in there. Did Perry tote the water for you?"

"Nope, I heated it myself. Mind you, it was a shallow bath, but it sure felt good."

"So you didn't see anyone for a while. What else?"

"Jerri hollered at me through the door that she'd found some jeans she could wear, but she had to put a hem in them. I think she was going to look for a needle and thread."

"Yes, yes, I heard that. And then Perry accused her of snooping through his things."

"They had a few words about it, but she assured him she had no interest in his silly suitcase."

"Okay then, what about Simmons?"

"He made himself scarce most of the morning, but he kept the fire going in the basement furnace, that's all I cared about. It's a big house, Sable. Four people can avoid each other for a long time." She sat on the bed while Sable changed into the scrub pants. "Lie down and keep that ice on your head. We need to watch you for the next few hours."

Sable sighed. "I know the drill."

* * *

Craig slid a plate across the dining table toward Murph and lifted the lid from the roasting pot, allowing the aroma to fill the room. "Are you going to tell me what's going on in this house, Murph, or am I going to have to go upstairs and bully Sable?"

Murph shoved the plate away. He wasn't hungry. "Someone attacked us."

The lid clattered to the table.

Murph glanced toward the door. "I'd appreciate it if you didn't say anything about this to the others. Someone must have followed us. We were looking at the crystal cavern when that natural bridge seemed to crumble on top of us. Someone had been hiding there."

"No idea who?"

"None. Sable was in front of me, and we both got shoved toward the pit. The ledge collapsed beneath her, and I couldn't hold on to her."

Craig shoved the pot aside and leaned over the table. "First, Sable wrecks her car down in Oklahoma, then—"

"Keep your voice down."

"Next," Craig said more softly, "she nearly falls into the ravine." In spite of Murph's warning, the volume rose again with every word. "Then someone tries to drown Simmons in the creek."

"Maybe not. Please lower your voice. I'd like to know what he was doing out there in the first place."

"Is Audry still upstairs with Sable?"

Murph nodded. If Boswell had wanted to fool everyone—if, indeed, Boswell was behind this—Audry would be a good choice. She may behave like a kind, talkative woman, mature in years, but she was in good physical condition, and she was sharp.

The door opened and Bryce entered the kitchen. "I tried to check on Sable, but Audry wouldn't let me in. Any food left?"

Murph slid his unused plate, fork and knife across the table. "Plenty. Have some."

Bryce took a seat across from Murph and reached for the pot. "I'm starved. Who cooked this?"

"I have no idea," Murph said.

"I need to go talk to Sable." Craig shoved his plate aside and left.

Sable had nearly fallen asleep when Craig arrived at her door, insisting that he had to talk to her alone.

After a brief run-in with Audry, he got his way. With a disapproving sigh, Audry walked out, leaving the door open. Sable motioned for Craig to close it as he entered.

"What's so important you had to disturb me from my death bed?" she drawled.

Craig did as she directed and sank onto the chest at the end of the bed. "Someone tries to kill you what, twice? Three times? And you don't think it's important?"

Sable groaned and readjusted the ice pack. "What did Murph say?"

"I want to know what *you* say. You can't just leave everybody in the dark like this. Something big's going on, and that means everyone in this house could be in danger."

"I'm sorry. Apparently, someone followed us from Freemont."

"And that's important because…?"

She stifled a groan. She didn't have the energy for another explanation. "That's what we're here to find out."

"Sable, has it ever occurred to you that Murph is the one who followed you? Doesn't it strike you as strange that—"

"Someone tried to kill Murph." Sometimes Craig Holt was the most annoying…

"What!"

"Keep your voice down! We're trying to keep this from making the papers this afternoon, if you don't mind. It happened on the hillside while he was chopping wood yesterday. You saw his injury. I saw it happen, but again, I didn't see who. Now stop with the brother act."

Craig spread his hands and stood up. "Fine." He paced to the window, arms folded across his chest. "Something's up, and you don't think I deserve an explanation. What did the police tell you about Josiah's automobile accident?"

She hesitated at the abrupt change of subject. "They thought he might have fallen asleep at the wheel, or swerved to miss an animal on the road, and his truck went off the road."

"And that's what they told you killed him."

"He hit a tree."

Craig was silent for a moment, arms stiffly folded over his chest, face grim. "Josiah didn't have any automobile accident," he said softly. "That wasn't what killed him."

"What are you talking about?"

"There's something else you need to know. Something only the mortician would see."

"You mean Bobby Ray?"

"Yes, but he'd get into big trouble if anyone found out."

"Let's hear it."

Bryce carried his dishes to the sink. "Murph, were you and Craig fighting when I came in?"

"No, we're both just a little jumpy after Sable's accident."

"Good." Bryce grinned as he returned to the table. "So don't get mad at him, okay? He played the same trick on me that Sable played on her brothers."

"What trick?"

"He left me alone in the cave."

"He *left* you?"

"He kept aiming his flashlight at the ceiling of the passage, like he was looking for something specific. You know where all that fog got so thick? We came to a little stream of water trickling from up above. He climbed up the side and disappeared into that fog. After awhile I called to him, but he didn't answer. He'd just disappeared."

"He never told you what he was searching for?"

"Nope. That guy loves to get dirty. Did you see all that mud on him?"

"How long was he gone?"

"Maybe ten or fifteen minutes. I had a flashlight, could've found my way back, but I decided to stay put."

Murph shoved his chair backward. "I need to check on Sable."

"Hey, wait, I didn't think you'd get mad at him!" Bryce called.

The ice pack was getting warm, and Sable needed to refill it. She also needed to use the restroom and get a drink of water. But not before she heard what Craig had to say.

"Better be sure you want to hear this," Craig said, "because you won't like it. I swear it's the truth, though. Bobby Ray wouldn't lie about this."

"Craig, just tell me."

He took a deep breath, reached up to comb his fingers through his damp black hair. "Bobby was supposed to keep the casket closed, right?"

"Yes. The body was prepared in Freemont. There wasn't any reason for him to do anything."

"He always respects the family's wishes. He's a good mortician."

"Craig, what did Bobby Ray do?"

"The coroner in Freemont called him after the body was shipped, reminding him not to open the casket under any circumstances." His voice grew louder as he talked.

"And?"

"Why would he have made such a point about that?"

Sable glanced toward the closed door. "Craig, lower your voice."

He turned from his vigil at the window and leaned so close to Sable she could smell the roast beef and onions on his breath. "What were you told about the body?"

"The coroner advised a closed casket because of the damage."

"There wasn't a mark on Josiah's body."

The soggy ice pack fell from Sable's hands.

"I convinced Bobby Ray to open the casket," he said.

"Against the wishes of the family? Craig—"

"Remember it was Bobby Ray's son who was with me when…when I had that wreck that got me into such hot water. Bobby Ray knew about Boswell's blackmail of Dad, and since then he's never trusted Boswell, either. We agreed it might be helpful to just see why the Freemont coroner had insisted on a closed casket. I mean, I've practically been a member of this family, and I didn't feel everything was just right, you know?"

"Why were you suspicious?"

"I knew Josiah wanted to talk to Dad about contacting the legislators in Oklahoma about some mining discrepancies."

"Discrepancies?"

"Ground pollution. Contamination from the mine tailings. Right now there isn't a lot of legislation to control the mining companies, and the unethical drillers tend to swoop in, tear up the land, swoop back out, leaving millions of dollars worth of cleanup that they don't have to answer for. You can bet Boswell would take advantage of that loophole if he could."

"Grandpa was worried about this pollution?"

Craig nodded. "You know if Boswell found out Josiah talked to Dad, he pitched a fit."

"Craig, are you suggesting he killed Grandpa to stop—"

"Josiah's body didn't have a mark on it, no bruises, no blood. Does that sound like he died in a car wreck? Why manipulate to have a closed casket when there was no reason for it? But Bobby Ray had his orders, and he could get into big trouble for taking the risk he did."

"That's why he didn't say anything to any of the family at the funeral."

"Sable, a body doesn't bruise after it's dead, isn't that right? And your grandfather was in a wreck. So, it means he was already dead when the wreck happened. Looks to me like the wreck was staged to cover up that somebody killed Josiah. I'm betting Boswell was in on it. Josiah thought he'd gotten such a good deal when he and his buddy Noah bought into the mine in Freemont."

Craig sat down beside her. "Now are you going to tell me what's going on around—"

The door flew open and Murph strode into the room, eyes blazing fury. "Get away from her."

TWENTY-THREE

It had been a long time since Murph had felt such an urge to punch someone. Apparently, his face reflected his feelings, because as he started across the room at Craig, Sable scrambled from the bed.

"Murph, what are you doing?"

"I said, get away from her." When Craig didn't move, Murph reached beneath his shirt.

"No!" Sable cried. "Murph, please, what are you doing?"

Murph didn't take his gaze from Craig. "Why did you leave Bryce alone in that passage?"

Craig groaned and rolled his eyes. "Bryce told you about that? Look, it was no big deal, okay?"

"What did you do with the watch?"

"What are you talking about?" Sable asked.

"That's what I'd like to know," Craig said. "You're losing it, pal. I mean, you're really losing it here."

"Our attacker took the watch and chain from Sable's neck."

Confusion filled Craig's face. "That old thing? Why?"

"Good question," Murph said. "Sable told you just before we separated down in the cave that her watch didn't run."

"And that's supposed to make me want to steal it?"

"If you knew *why* it didn't work," Murph said.

"Like I should care? I knew it was a sentimental thing for her. It was Josiah's watch. Besides how am I supposed to have attacked you and taken Sable's watch when I was halfway on the other side of the whole cave system?"

"You left Bryce alone in that passage," Murph said. "You know the cave as well as anyone. If there's a shortcut to the crystal cavern—"

"You're trying to say you think I pushed you?" Craig exclaimed.

"We were the only four down there."

"Man, you're crazy!"

"Why did you leave Bryce alone in that passage?" Murph asked again.

"We were looking for the sinkhole Josiah fell into last fall, right? Naturally, when the fog thickened, I thought for sure there was an opening nearby—you know, dry, cold air mingled with warmer, moist air from the cave." He glanced at Sable, and in spite of Murph's current grilling, Craig's eyes glinted with triumph. "I found it."

"What?" Sable exclaimed. "The sinkhole?"

Craig shrugged. "Doesn't amount to much, and I couldn't get out because the hole was about four feet above my head." He looked back at Murph. "Are you satisfied?"

"Why couldn't you have told Bryce that?" Sable asked.

"Oh, come on, Sable, if I'd have told Bryce, he'd have blabbed it to you, and—"

"Stop with the silly games," Murph said. "You left a kid alone in the cave."

"Bryce laughed when we told him our stories," Craig said. "I thought he'd get a kick out of it, and then I'd get to tease Sable for months, because I knew something about the cave that she didn't know."

Murph leaned against the door frame and crossed his arms over his chest. Craig Holt was a big kid. A goof.

Right now Murph was beginning to feel like a goof, himself. So much for logical conclusions.

Sable sank back onto the bed and picked up the ice pack. "Craig, would you mind filling this with ice again?"

"Um, sure, no problem. Are you sure you're safe with this lunatic?"

"I'll be fine."

Murph sank onto the chest when Craig walked out. "Sorry. It was too great a coincidence to ignore."

Sable chuckled.

"It isn't funny," he said.

She laughed out loud, then immediately groaned and reached for her head. "I wish I'd had a camera. My brothers will love hearing about this."

He knew he shouldn't allow his masculine pride to be offended. "I nearly pulled my gun. I don't think it's funny."

"I'm sorry." She made an obvious effort to adjust her expression. "Okay, granted, you don't know Craig the way I do, but it's just like him to look for that sinkhole and then try to keep it a secret."

Murph had to agree with her. Craig had never grown up.

She got up from the bed and closed the door, then sat back down. "Murph, I don't believe in ghosts."

He blinked, mystified.

"But I don't know how else to explain what happened down there," she said. "How does anyone see without any kind of light?"

"Ah, the ghost eyes. I thought your head injury might be severe when you said that. It scared me. But the 'ghost' took your watch."

"There was no flashlight, nothing but this sort of intermittent green glow. I thought I was going to be strangled, but the attacker just broke the chain, took the watch and left."

Murph reached for the flashlight on her dresser. "Could you have had some kind of temporary blindness?"

"A reaction to the concussion? I suppose. I don't know any other way to explain it."

"Are you having any trouble with your vision now?"

"None. Why would anyone take my watch?"

"I don't know, unless the attacker had a reason to believe

there was something important in it. The only person who knows it doesn't work, aside from you and me, is Craig."

"And Bryce. A couple of kids. But also, the map had a drawing of the watch face next to the etching of the sinkhole, and someone took that map. Maybe someone made the connection."

He shone a beam into her right eye, then her left. "Pupils equal and reactive. Do you know what day it is?"

"Sunday."

"Your age?"

"I'll be thirty-one on Tuesday."

"Where are we?"

"Missouri Ozarks. I can see you, I'm alert and oriented."

He put the flashlight back on the dresser.

"Grandpa was murdered," Sable said quietly.

Murph frowned at her. "Well, we had considered that, of course, but what makes you think it's true?"

"Craig told me."

"*Craig?* How would he know?"

"He saw Grandpa's body after it arrived back here for burial."

"And he saw something suspicious?"

"Our family was advised to have a closed casket," Sable explained, "but Craig said there wasn't a mark on the body." She leaned forward. "Murph, we can trust Craig. I believe him."

There was a knock at the door. Murph stiffened. "Yes?"

"Room service, with the ice the lady ordered."

Murph opened the door, and Craig brought in two plastic zipper bags filled with broken pieces of ice from outside. He presented them to Sable with a flourish.

Sable took them and nodded to Murph. "Close the door. He needs to know what's going on. Craig, we need to talk."

Sable let Murph feed Craig information in sound bites. Craig's dark brows drew closer with each revelation, until they formed a slash across his forehead. She knew that look well.

"So you're wanted by the police," he said to Sable when

Murph had finished his story. "They're blaming you for the murder of Murph's uncle?"

"That's right," Sable said.

"Morons," he muttered. "You should tell the others."

"One of those others obviously followed us from Freemont," Murph said.

"But the rest didn't. Shouldn't they be warned?"

"About what?" Murph asked. "Only Sable and I are being stalked."

"Look, all I'm saying here is that I'm sure glad you told *me,* okay? Don't you think the others would appreciate it, too? They've got to know something's going on, anyway, with all the so-called accidents happening around here."

"Let's wait," Sable said. "The situation could get even further out of hand."

Craig shrugged and stood. "Fine with me, but I think you need more people to watch your backside, if you know what I mean. I'm going downstairs to check the fire."

When he left, Murph gestured to Sable. "Come to the attic with me? We need to find out what's in that safe. We must have missed a clue in Josiah's note."

Sable retrieved the note from the pocket of her discarded slacks. "I'm with you."

"Read the note to me again," Murph said. They were missing something, but he thought they were on the right track.

As she read it to him, he dialed the combination, convinced that the note referred to something more sinister than Josiah's involvement with the Seitz mine.

Why would anyone salt the crystal cavern? It didn't make sense. It wasn't as if Josiah was going to sell it as a mining site. Why would he have had those chunks of galena, sphalerite and silver analyzed?

Murph tried the handle. Nothing.

"Okay," Sable said, "Try again, but this time only spin the dial once after fifteen. He might not have realized he was suggesting twice."

Murph followed her directions. This time the metal handle slid up stiffly.

"It worked!" He swung the thick door open.

The shelves were crammed with papers—birth certificates, marriage licenses, property titles.

Sable pulled out a folder marked Photographs. She thumbed through the first few, holding them up to the glow from Murph's flashlight.

"It looks like the crystal cavern," Murph said. "Why would he have photographed that?"

She turned the snapshot over. Josiah had written "Seitz mine" in his flamboyant script on the back.

She held up the next photo. "*This* one is the crystal cavern."

"Then what's this?" Murph asked, picking up the next one on the stack. He read it and whistled again. "That's Number Three, one of the working mines outside of Freemont. It looks as if he was comparing the places."

She held the three photos up together. "These are all dated in January this year. What do you think about this, Murph? He checked the Seitz mine that Boswell had convinced him and Noah to purchase. Maybe he had the ore from there analyzed, compared it to an existing analysis of Number Three, and found them to be too similar. Then he came home and figured out how to salt the cavern below, just to see if it looked similar to the Seitz mine. That's something Grandpa would do."

Murph was impressed. "I think that sounds like a plausible explanation, and much more acceptable than taking this note at face value."

They sorted through more papers, then pulled out a thick manila folder labeled Boswell Enterprises, Inc.

Murph peered over her shoulder. "I didn't know Boswell had another corporation."

She opened the folder and found a stack of photocopies.

Murph recognized the form—it was the workers' compensation report, prepared by the clinic doctors. There was a sticky note at the bottom of each copy. *Not filed. Not filed. Not filed.*

Sable shuffled through the pages until she came to a sheet with her signature at the bottom.

"So these weren't turned in," Murph said.

"You asked me about that," Sable said. "You were right."

He had never been less pleased to have his instincts validated. "The workers must have been paid by the company, or there'd have been an outcry for lost wages."

Sable thumbed through several other pages with notes jotted in Josiah's distinctive handwriting. "Craig told me Boswell has resorted to blackmail in the past. This looks like Grandpa was tracking everything in Boswell's dealings that wasn't kosher." She handed the copy to Murph and held the next page to the light. "Look at this."

"It's a list of people who died from accidents in the past six years."

"Mining accidents?" she asked.

"No. There's a record of an automobile accident and a fall into a grain elevator."

"Here's the name of a friend of mine who worked in Boswell's office," Sable said. "She was supposed to have died in a car wreck."

Murph looked at the next stack of stapled pages, topped by a ledger sheet. Scrawled across the upper margin in Josiah's writing were the words *Special Ops.*

"Sable, this is why your grandfather and Noah died," Murph said softly. "Boswell must have learned Josiah was collecting information. I heard a rumor about a week after I started working at the clinic, but since it was from someone who was known as a notorious gossip, I dismissed it."

"Something else about Grandpa?"

"No. Did you ever meet the doctor you replaced at the clinic?"

"Heidlage? I was told he retired."

"Who told you?"

"I think…Otis Boswell. Oh, no, don't tell me Heidlage died."

"He had complained about the number of mining accident victims presenting to the clinic. Then he attempted to standardize emergency procedures for mining accidents. He started researching the past accidents, even went so far as to visit one of the mines. He spoke to several of the ambulance personnel. Then, all of a sudden, he left."

"He quit? Or are you saying he was frightened off?"

"He gave notice and was gone in two weeks. He never explained why he was leaving."

"That was mentioned a couple of times in the office," Sable said, "but I didn't think much about it, either."

"Maybe it's something we need to think about," he suggested, thumbing through the workers' comp copies. "Have you noticed that none of these reports are about anything serious? Anyone wishing to prevent an investigation by OSHA would want to keep reports to a minimum, particularly the minor ones that could be paid out of company coffers."

"I haven't heard many complaints about the safety conditions," Sable said. "But Boswell's miners get good pay, better than many other miners in the country. For that much money, they'll keep their mouths shut."

"Someone at the clinic might even have been paid to pull the reports filed by the medical staff," Murph said. "And Josiah found this out. Who knows, maybe Heidlage even revealed it to him, since Josiah was one of Boswell's partners. That could be when Josiah began to check things out a little more closely."

Sable touched the lump on her head. "So we're in danger because Grandpa was trying to uphold the law, not break it."

"Sounds likely. Still think you can handle a gun?"

"Yes."

"Could you shoot someone if you had to?"

She hesitated. "Could you?"

"I worked as a medic for a mining company that had holdings in Colombia. They sent me there once, armed to protect myself against drug runners operating nearby. We...had a run-in. It was either shoot or be shot. I didn't kill, but I did maim. I'll never forget it, Sable. Believe me, shooting a human being isn't easy. What if our killer turns out to be Jerri? Or Craig?"

She closed her eyes.

He drew her closer. "We've found what we're looking for."

"We'll never get out of here with it."

"I'm the pessimist here, remember?"

"All of a sudden everything's changed."

He felt the soft warmth of her breath against his cheek. "I know. I have even more reason to want to live now."

She rested her forehead against his shoulder.

"This could become addictive," Murph said.

"You mean the terror of running for our lives?"

"I mean learning to depend on each other."

"Sable!" came a sharp female voice from below. "Sable Chamberlin? Are you okay?" It was Audry. Time to go.

TWENTY-FOUR

That evening, oil lamps flickered on the shelves of the upper hallway, and a scent of vanilla drifted through the air. Flames danced downstairs in the fireplace beneath a mantel decorated with three glowing candles. The house radiated warmth. Audry and Jerri had done a good job.

Sable walked down the stairway beside Murph. Except for a lingering headache, she felt physically well. The strange and frightening episode of blindness had not recurred.

Special Ops.

"I'm not hungry," she muttered to Murph.

"You haven't eaten since breakfast. You'll feel better with something in your stomach, and Audry says there's a surprise for dinner."

"Are we ready for another surprise?" *Mining accidents.*

His hand tightened on her arm, and he stopped and turned to her. "Speaking of surprises, maybe Craig is right about telling the others. This situation is getting out of hand. It isn't right to withhold information from those who could be affected."

"As you said, it's not right to endanger their lives." *Unfiled workers' comp reports.*

"Consider this. Your grandfather collected all the evidence against Boswell without telling you what he was up to. He wanted to protect you, but by trying to protect you, he ultimately placed you in more danger."

"I understand what you're saying, but this is different. If we announce there's a stalker among us, we'll be alerting the stalker, as well. Let's see what happens tonight."

They entered the kitchen, where Audry and Perry stood at the stove disagreeing amiably about the seasonings, while Bryce and Craig sat at the dining table discussing their excursion into the cave this morning. Simmons sat at the end of the table with his back to the wall, silent.

"How's the goose egg on your hand?" Craig asked Sable as she took a seat across from him.

"It's more of a hen egg than a goose egg now," she said.

Audry came to the table with a huge covered platter. She set it on the table and stepped back. "You won't believe who cooked tonight's dinner." She gestured grandly toward Perry Chadwick, who stood beside the kitchen counter. "Our water carrier. He's a chef, complete with cookbooks! He was on his way to a chef's challenge cook-off at Big Cedar."

"Big Cedar, huh?" Jerri leaned back to get a better look at Perry, her red hair gleaming bronze in the candlelight. "Is there a cooking contest in a resort in the middle of winter?"

Perry nodded. "Covered live by Springfield's Channel 33. If I win, I travel to St. Louis for the regional next month."

Jerri glanced at Simmons. "And you're on your way to Harrison, Arkansas?"

"Not by choice," the man grumbled. "My mom's in Fayetteville, but my sister wants me to go to her house in Harrison, get her car and drive it to Fayetteville. That's how I got into this crazy situation in the first place."

Sable exchanged glances with Murph. Simmons wasn't on the wrong bus.

Audry whisked the cover from the large platter of food. "Venison with mushroom sauce, garlic potato pancakes, green beans with herbed almonds, handmade croissants."

Perry pulled off his apron and held a chair for Audry. "Time to dine."

As the others passed the gourmet fare around the table, Sable sipped her water, studying her guests.

Audry beamed at Perry, as if he were her own chick just hatched. "You could have told me you were a chef."

Perry chuckled. "I'm an amateur. I have a lot to learn."

Jerri served herself and passed the platter. "An amateur is someone who does something simply for the love of it."

Perry patted his belly. "Guilty as charged."

"Now, Perry, don't be too hard on yourself," Audry chided. "I bet you've built up some muscle carrying all that water."

"Your coordination is improving, too," Jerri observed. "I watched you carry wood in from the pile beside the front porch, and you didn't fall on the ice."

Perry served himself small portions. "I'm not doing as well as Craig, though. He practically skated all the way to the bridge and back today."

Simmons looked up from his food. "The bridge?"

"I thought we might have to get Sable to a hospital after her fall," Craig said. "The ice is thick, and the bridge tilts dangerously. It would have to be cleared before we can leave."

"We seldom used that bridge," Sable said. "It's so much farther out that way."

"But not as steep," Craig said. "The bridge is the most dangerous part. I thought I might go out and try my hand at chopping after dinner."

"Who said anything about leaving?" Simmons asked.

Craig gave Sable a pointed look. She held his gaze.

"I'm not going anywhere on this ice," Audry announced. "I've had too many bad weather experiences in these Ozark hills. We simply can't afford any more emergencies."

"Sable, are you sure you're doing okay?" Jerri asked. "If we need to get you to medical care—"

"It's a possibility," she said. "I seemed to have some visual disturbances earlier, when I was in the cave."

"Somebody else was down there," Bryce said slowly. "I heard you, Murph. You told Craig somebody attacked you."

The room fell into stunned silence.

"Attacked?" Audry cried.

There was a moment of cacophony as several voices were raised at once. The dinner was forgotten.

"Please, everyone calm down." Murph's deep voice rose above the din. "We did have an extra spelunker down in the cave this morning." He described the incident briefly. "It's possible someone was exploring the pit and didn't want to be disturbed. When we arrived, whoever it was might have felt it was necessary to jump us, to get away unseen."

Perry set his water glass down with a clatter. "That's drastic action just to avoid being identified as a trespasser."

Simmons looked from face to face around the table, eyes narrowed to slits, face paling.

"Is there another entrance to the cave?" Jerri asked. "Surely it couldn't have been one of us...."

"Tell them, Sable," Craig said. "They know this much, they need to know it all."

She could have cut a hole through Craig with her glare, but he wouldn't drop his gaze.

"Sable?" Jerri said. "Is there something else going on?"

"Someone also pushed Sable over the side of the cliff the other night," Craig said. "She didn't slip on the ice. And that 'accident' Murph had in the woods yesterday was no accident. Sable saw someone throw a log at him."

"Sable?" Audry said. "Why didn't you say anything earlier?"

"Sable and I didn't want to alarm everyone," Murph said. "And we knew someone was dangerous, but we didn't know who."

"And you do now?" Audry asked, glancing around the table.

"No, we don't." Sable tucked her napkin beneath the edge of her plate. "It could be anyone here. We can't go into great detail now, but it seems someone followed us here to stop us from finding evidence about crimes committed in Freemont."

"Murders," Craig added.

"Stop it!" Sable told him. "You're making it worse."

"There's been too much covered up already," Craig said.

"Murders!" Audry exclaimed. "Are you saying Josiah was murdered?"

Sable's glare found a new target. The woman used Grandpa's name with far too much familiarity.

"Please," Murph said, "if you've seen anything that might help, tell Sable or me. Tell all of us, in fact, right now. From here on out, now that the danger is known, we must take every precaution until we leave here."

"We should all stay close to one another," Sable said. "And we should lock our bedroom doors at night."

"Oh, that's just great," Perry spluttered. "We're stuck in the middle of the woods, possibly with a murderer. Where am I supposed to sleep? There's no lock on my door, remember? I'm alone in the sewing room. What am I supposed to do?"

"Stay in the room with Simmons and me," Murph said.

Dinner ended on that note.

TWENTY-FIVE

Sable picked up a glowing oil lamp from a mirrored shelf in the dining room. "Audry, may I speak with you for a moment?" Without waiting for a reply, she led the way across the hall and into the cozy family room, where bookcases lined the walls and the darkened television hovered in a far corner. She placed the lamp on a table along the wall and closed the door behind the slender, gray-haired woman...the woman with suddenly watchful eyes.

Sable pulled the old photograph of Audry, Grandpa and Otis Boswell from the pocket of her jeans and held it out. "You never told me you knew my grandfather. I'm curious why."

Audry slowly took the snapshot from Sable's fingers and studied it. She closed her eyes for a second, then opened them and met Sable's gaze. "I'm sorry, honey. I'm...it seems you've caught me off guard."

"How?" By the expression on Audry's face, Sable could tell she wouldn't want to know the answer to her questions, and yet she couldn't *not* ask.

"Believe me," Audry said, "if I knew anything that could help, I'd be the first to tell you."

Sable waited.

Audry turned to gaze around the room. She stepped over to a game table between two chairs. "All these furnishings are different from how it looked years ago."

"You were a friend of my grandparents?"

Audry shook her head. "I never knew your grandmother. I was here only once." She turned again to face Sable. "Your grandfather was a wonderful man."

"How well did you know him? I need to know. This could be very important."

Audry stepped once more to the window. "Josiah and I were... good friends once. Can we leave it at that?"

For a long moment, Sable forgot to breathe. "No, we can't. I need to know as much as possible about my grandfather and Otis Boswell. Why were you photographed with them?"

Audry handed the photo back to Sable. "This was a fluke. I worked at a café in Cassville to supplement my teaching salary. I was a widow raising two teenagers. That picture of the three of us was probably taken after a high school ball game. I often saw both of them at the school athletics events."

"So you didn't know Otis well?"

"He came to the café a couple of times when Josiah was there. Craig's father, Reuben Holt, frequented the café, as well."

"You knew Reuben?"

"I knew many of the locals. It's a tight community, you know. The men would sit together many mornings at the café. I'd pour them coffee and try to interest them in breakfast to improve business. I taught their kids in school."

"So you weren't all the best of friends?"

"Far from it."

"But you and my grandfather were," Sable said.

Audry didn't meet her gaze. She sighed. "I'll tell you this only because of the current extreme circumstances. I apologize first, because this is going to hurt like fire, but I...I guess you should know." She looked at Sable, then turned away. "I was a lonely widow who had been married too long to an abusive alcoholic. I knew your grandmother worked long hours at her restaurant in Eureka Springs, and Josiah was lonely. Our friendship became intimate one afternoon."

Sable thought she'd been prepared, but she hadn't. The pain

of her grandfather's betrayal shot through her like a hot knife. For a moment, she squeezed her eyes shut and clamped her teeth together to keep from crying out. How much more was she going to discover before this whole, ugly episode ended?

Audry continued, her voice soft, filled with sorrow. "Only once, Sable. Afterward, we were both remorseful. It never happened again. As I told you, your grandfather was a good man, and he regretted his one lapse. He loved your grandmother, and he loved your mother very much."

"Obviously not enough to resist temptation." Sable couldn't keep the bitterness from her voice. She bit her lip and crossed her arms over her chest.

"Otis Boswell found out, somehow," Audry said. "I don't know how. But I do know Josiah was always afraid Otis would use that knowledge to his own advantage."

"Did he?" Sable asked.

Audry spread her hands. "I never knew. I got a teaching job in Sedalia the following year, and left the area, because I knew my own weakness. You see, honey, I loved Josiah more than I've ever loved another man. It was too painful to stay."

There was a sharp rap on the door and Audry fell silent.

It was Craig. "Did Jerri come in here with you two? Murph and I can't find her."

It was decided that while Murph searched for Jerri, everyone else would congregate in the family room, an uncomfortable arrangement for all, but the safest.

Audry distracted Bryce with a game of Scrabble while Simmons, Perry and Craig eyed each other with suspicion.

Sable stood at the window, overlooking the bridge that Craig had inspected for crossing. Her pain over Grandpa's infidelity converged with her fear that was foremost over all.

Was Audry telling the truth? Sable had already jumped to too many conclusions about Grandpa's transgressions. Should she believe he cheated on his wife just because a woman—who had been a stranger two days ago—claimed an affair with him?

But what motive would Audry have for lying?

Sable's every nerve attuned to the sounds in the room, hearing each inflection of voice as the men speculated about Jerri's whereabouts.

"She was going to the basement to add wood to the heating stove," Perry said. "She left the basement door open."

"She wasn't there when I looked," Craig said.

"So you say." Simmons growled aggressively, perhaps to disguise his fear.

Sable continued to listen for any note of falseness, aware that her reading of their voices could be colored by her own fear. They were all trapped. The stalker who had followed her and Murph had boxed them all in.

Conversely, their stalker was also cornered, and cornered predators could be dangerous.

She desperately needed some time alone.

Murph could accurately say that he'd been developing a much closer relationship with God in the past couple of days. He prayed with every step he took.

The lamps still burned in the upstairs hallway, so Murph didn't need a flashlight. He would feel better as soon as he found Jerri. There was no sign of her in the basement, and he knew she wouldn't set foot in the cave.

He expected to find her sleeping somewhere, but so far he hadn't come upon her. He'd seen her conked out on the sofa twice today, and she'd barely stayed awake during their meals. The woman seemed to be so thoroughly sleep-deprived and she could snooze through a tornado. In spite of the danger she'd just learned about, it was possible she had come upstairs for a nap. After all, she probably concluded that she wasn't being stalked.

He stepped to Sable's door, knocked, opened it. Empty. Methodically, he checked the other rooms. Dillon followed his every step.

When Murph returned to the hallway, inspection completed, he noticed the attic door standing ajar. Dillon's ears perked forward, and he whined. He walked up to Murph and nosed his hand, then whined again.

"What is it?"

The dog led the way up the attic steps, scratched at the door, opening it further with his nose.

Moments later, Murph found Jerri. How he wished she'd just been sleeping.

TWENTY-SIX

"Gotcha!"

Loud laughter echoed through the room. Sable jerked around to find Bryce shaking his hands over his head in a victorious wave. "Two out of three, Audry. You'd better start brushing up on your vocabulary."

Audry pushed her chair back from the table. "I think you need to get Perry over here, you cocky little—"

Murph rushed in through the family room door, his expression grim. He looked at Sable.

Everyone fell silent.

"Well?" Perry asked.

Murph paused for breath. "I found Jerri."

"What do you mean you *found* her?" Audry asked softly.

"She's upstairs in the attic." Again, his eyes sought Sable's. "She's dead."

Shocked silence rocked the room, and with that silence crept the specter of death—and dread that it might suddenly have become contagious.

Sable knew too well about that contagion.

"When was she last seen?" Audry asked.

"I saw her go downstairs to stoke the fire," Perry said. "Murph…how did it happen?"

"Wait a minute," Murph said. "Before we discuss this, Craig, you need to put whatever chains or studded tires or whatever you can find onto that Jeep. We've got to get out of here. *Now.*"

"And get ourselves killed in the process?" Perry exclaimed.

"That road isn't any less dangerous now than it was when we arrived here, when we couldn't even walk on it, much less drive."

"What killed her?" Sable asked Murph. "I need to go see—"

Murph stopped her at the threshold. "Not yet. There's a bullet hole in her head."

"A bullet!" Audry cried. "Oh, no." She raised her hand to her face. Her eyes closed, and she swayed. "No. This can't be happening."

Sable grabbed Audry by the arm and eased her down into the nearest chair.

"Someone shot her?" Bryce asked. "But we didn't hear any—"

"I agree with Murph," Craig said. "We need to get out of here. I can scrounge up some chains in the garage to fit my Jeep. I'll warn you, though, the tires will still slide on the thick ice out there. We'll have to take the back road that's less steep. That bridge still needs some deicing. I think chopping at it should be our first job."

Audry covered her face with her hands. "Oh, poor Jerri. I can't believe this is happening." Her shoulders shook.

"Are you sure she's dead?" Bryce asked Murph.

"I'm sure," Murph said.

Simmons stood up from his chair. "How do we know we can trust what you say, Murph?"

"How long has she been dead?" Bryce asked. "When did it—"

"We're all gonna die right here in this house," Audry moaned.

"We've got to not panic, to slow down and think rationally." Murph snapped, "Craig, get the chains on your Jeep."

"I need to chop the ice on the bridge."

"I can help you with both," Murph said.

"We all can help," Bryce said.

"You're not serious about leaving tonight, are you?" Perry exclaimed.

"Why do you want us to stay?" Simmons said scornfully, glowering at the chubby man. "What good's it gonna do you if we all die here?"

"That won't happen if we can help it," Murph said. "We're going to get out of here."

* * *

Murph was loath to leave Jerri's body lying alone in the cold attic, but there was no choice. The scene of the crime had to remain intact, and the group needed to get out and call for help.

He only prayed no one else would be injured before they could escape.

Murph wasn't a policeman; he didn't know the correct procedure, wasn't sure what to do next—but then, he doubted many people in this same situation would be prepared.

"Craig, you're the best on ice, I think," he said. "We need you to take the pickax out and start on that bridge."

"I've been working on that some already," Craig said.

"Good. We'll bring out some coals from the furnace to help melt the ice, too."

"How do you know you can trust Craig?" Simmons demanded. "We let him out of our sight, he could—"

"You and I will go with him," Murph said.

"Fine, then we'll take the coals with us as we go."

"What about me?" Bryce asked. "I can help, too."

"You can stay here with Perry and the women." Simmons grabbed his jacket from a hook by the back door. "I want out of here."

"Right," Craig said. "The axes are on the front porch. Find another flashlight and watch your footing. It'll be treacherous out there."

Craig opened the back door and stepped onto the patio. Simmons filled a bucket with ashes from the fireplace, and followed him.

Murph leaned close to Sable, brushed her hair back and whispered in her ear. "Get the .22 pistol out of the hunting closet. Take care of yourself. Remember what you said to me down in the cave yesterday?"

"I said lots of things."

"You said you didn't think you could stand it if anything happened to me." He lowered his lips to hers in a brief, gentle kiss. "Be careful. Don't let anything happen to you, because I honestly can't see myself without you. The moon is bright. Keep watch out the family room window, and if you see anything go wrong, get the others out of this house." He opened the door and stepped out into the cold stillness.

As soon as he disappeared into the night, Sable raced up the stairs. Loading the pistol she'd used so many times for target practice, she couldn't help wondering about the questions Murph had asked her earlier: Would she be able to bring herself to shoot someone? Could she take a human life? And if not, would someone she loved die because of it?

The moon glared from a star-studded sky, and the brightness was helpful. A cold wind blew a feathery cloud across the moon. Murph turned to gaze back through the leafless branches at the silent house. He didn't see Sable watching from the door, but then the curtain lifted at the long window of the family room, and her shadow-silhouette appeared. Reluctantly, he began walking beside Simmons.

Before he reached the bridge, he heard a familiar thunk, the stroke of an ax breaking ice. Moonlight outlined Craig laboring at the far end of the bridge.

"Could you use some help?" Murph called.

"Grab the pickax," Craig said without breaking his rhythm. "It's chipping away pretty well. Got those ashes, Simmons?"

"Right here," Simmons said. Instead of carrying the bucket across the bridge, he set it down beside him, then stepped around Murph.

"There's a gravel pile near the house, where Josiah was going to put in a driveway but never got around to it," Craig said. "We can use that for traction on any rough spots."

"There aren't going to be any rough spots for you two."

Murph frowned, turned and found himself staring down a gleaming gun barrel.

Craig's ax stilled.

"You shot her," Murph said.

Simmons smiled. "Is that really what you think?" His teeth looked wicked in the moonlight.

Murph didn't move, didn't reply.

"You two are working together, aren't you?" Simmons said. "You and Craig. I should've picked up on that yesterday when you went traipsing off into the cave together. You're covering each other."

Murph continued watching the barrel of the gun, as if it were a snake ready to strike. "What are you talking about?"

"I know what you're up to. You think you're going to have me all trussed up for the police. Who better to blame? The kid? Oh, yeah, he's scary. Or maybe it's the old lady, or the fat clown who can't even step out on the front porch without busting his face."

"Don't underestimate people," Murph said. "Where did you get the gun?"

"That isn't your business, is it?"

"You carry a gun to your mother's deathbed?"

There was a whisper of sound behind Murph, and Simmons redirected his aim. His shadowed face revealed little in the dim light of the moon. Unfortunately, his back was to the house, and Murph knew that even if Sable could see them, she couldn't tell what was happening.

"Don't come any closer," Simmons told Murph, "or your buddy's going to join Jerri in the grave."

"What are you *doing* with that thing?" Craig exclaimed.

Murph reached for his own weapon beneath his shirt, but Simmons brought his gun barrel hard against the side of Murph's head.

He struck again, and Murph sank to his knees as the night around him grew darker. He heard gunfire.

Then the blackness was complete.

TWENTY-SEVEN

"Murph's been shot!" Sable turned from the window and raced toward the back door.

Audry, Perry and Bryce joined her.

"What happened?" Audry pulled back the curtain over the door's central window.

Sable couldn't see much in the darkness, but she did see Simmons standing over Murph. Craig was on his side near the water's edge.

"Could be Simmons got both of them!" Audry exclaimed.

"I heard only one shot," Sable said.

"You know what this means, don't you?" Perry said. "Simmons is our guy."

"I never did like his attitude," Audry said.

"Murph and Craig need help," Sable said. "But you three need to get to safety."

"We're not leaving you here alone to face that goon," Perry said. "I heard you and Craig talk a lot about hunting, and that *was* venison I cooked that nobody ate tonight. There must be weapons somewhere in this house."

Sable considered the hunting closet, but she had no idea how familiar the others were with firearms. "How do you feel about a little cave exploration?" she asked.

"We can't leave Murph and Craig out there!" Audry exclaimed.

"I don't plan to, but the longer we stay here, the more opportunity Simmons has to hold us hostage. Bryce has had a tour of the cave system, and he might know another way out." She turned to Bryce. "Remember the breakdown cavern we went through this morning?"

The boy nodded. "I can find it."

"Good," Sable said. "I believe that gives us the advantage. Craig found a sinkhole there. It'll be our way out."

"There's a rope on the basement landing," Perry said, "and some flashlights."

"We'd better get a move on." Audry nudged Sable back down the hall. "Simmons could come back in here any second."

"I'm not going down yet," Sable said.

"Are you nuts?" Perry exclaimed. "Of course you're coming with us. Do you think Jerri's killer would hesitate to shoot you? Come on, Sable."

"I'll catch up with you."

"What are you going to do?" Perry asked.

"Take some precautions. Perry, take one of those garden spades with you. We may need to tunnel out. If I'm not down in five minutes, Bryce, take Perry and Audry on to the breakdown cavern. You can all hide in the rocks. It's a big room."

"I don't like this one bit," Audry said.

"I'll find you—promise." Sable nudged the group toward the basement door. "Now, go. Hurry."

"We'll be okay, Audry," Bryce assured the older woman. "Are you afraid of caves?"

"No, I'm afraid of killers."

As the others descended the basement steps, Sable ran up to the sewing room on the second floor. She checked the window, found it unlocked, shoved it open. If they needed an alternate entrance into the house later, this might provide one.

She was on her own.

Tentacles of fire shot across Murph's face and skull. He reached up and touched his injured jaw, tested the movement in his extremities and found nothing wrong, though his head shrieked with agony when he tried to sit up.

Someone kicked his left shoulder.

"Trying to make a run for it, Murphy?" Simmons mocked, leering down at him. "Want an extra hole in the head?"

Murph glared at the man's blurred, inverted image.

"Get up." Simmons shoved him again. "I'm not dragging you all the way to the house."

Murph glanced quickly around. From the corner of his eye, Murph saw Craig's prone body on a shadowy corner of the bridge.

He remembered the sound of a gunshot.

"Let's go," Simmons growled.

Murph climbed slowly to his feet, studying the gun in Simmons's hand. He prayed that Sable and the others had retreated to safety.

Lord, please don't let Sable try any heroics tonight. And please give me wisdom. Fast!

He paused and turned again to look at Craig's fallen body. "Aren't you even going to see if he's still alive?"

"I got him dead-on in the chest, and I'll do you the same favor if you don't get moving."

Oh, God, no! Not Craig. Murph had stared death in the face many times, but he'd never grown accustomed to it. This nightmare continued to spiral further out of control.

Simmons shoved him roughly. "I said get to the house!"

Murph turned away, but at the last second he thought he saw Craig's arm move. He looked toward the house and managed a step on the ice, then another. *Lord, please let him still be alive. Help me to get back to him.*

"Move!" Simmons shoved Murph with his free hand.

Murph continued unsteadily, praying for Craig, praying for Sable's safety, praying that the house would be empty when he and Simmons reached the back door.

"How does it feel to terrorize the same people who saved your life so recently?" Murph asked.

No answer.

"Doesn't it bother you? I mean, wondering what would have happened to you if Audry hadn't dragged you from the creek? If Sable and I hadn't performed CPR on you?"

"Shut up, or you'll find out it doesn't bother me to put a bullet in the back of your head."

Murph fell silent, but at the back door, he turned and faced Simmons, and once more found himself staring at the barrel of a gun—except this time he recognized the shape of his own Detonics in the glow of moonlight. It was a small six-shot semi-automatic pistol, and it looked like a toy in Simmons's beefy hand.

"One wrong move," Simmons said quietly, "and you're dead."

"And if we go inside, someone else will die. You'll just have to shoot me here."

Simmons kicked the door open with his right foot. It slammed against the inside wall with a crash of glass, inciting frantic barking from the depths of the house.

"Get inside!" Simmons shoved Murph forward.

Dillon came charging down the hallway.

"No, Dillon, stay!" Murph commanded the German shepherd.

The dog stopped in front of the open kitchen door, his hackles stiff, fangs bared in a snarl.

"Back, Dillon," Murph ordered.

Still growling, the dog backed into the kitchen.

Murph stepped inside, moving as slowly as he felt he could without provoking Simmons. He peered down the hallway. At first glance, the place seemed deserted, and he felt a wash of relief. Maybe everyone was safely out of the way.

Simmons followed Murph into the house, prodding him with the nose of the pistol. "Get into the living room."

Murph made his way there with Simmons following. Dillon continued to growl and back up as the two men advanced. As they stepped into the living room, Simmons took a wary glance at the basement door, which stood ajar, then motioned with the pistol for Murph to sit on the couch.

"Looks like your girlfriend left you to face the music alone," Simmons sneered. "That's fine with me. I bet she's told you everything I need to know."

Murph remained silent. Dillon took up a protective stance at the base of the stairwell.

A floorboard creaked on the second floor and Simmons shot a quick glance up to the landing. "Sounds like we might have some company," he said. "Back on your feet, Murphy. We're going on a little hunting trip."

Murph stood up and took a step toward Simmons, who kept the Detonics aimed steadily at Murph's chest.

"Stop!" Sable called from the top of the stairs.

Simmons shifted his aim.

Murph threw his weight at the other man's arm, driving it against the mantel of the fireplace. The pistol flew from Simmons's hand, clattering onto the hearth.

Simmons was reaching for his own gun when a shot rang out from the upstairs landing. The bullet from Sable's .22 ricocheted off the stone face of the hearth.

As Murph rolled to his left, Simmons scrambled to his feet and dived for the basement door. Sable squeezed off a second shot, taking a chunk of wood from the door, where the man's head had been a moment before.

"Murph!" Sable called as she rushed down the stairs and into his arms. "You're alive!"

He drew her close for a few seconds, and then she pulled away and looked up at him. "Craig?"

"I don't know. I think I saw him move, but Simmons thinks he's dead. I didn't want him to finish the job."

Murph listened at the basement. Had Simmons gone into the cave, or was he waiting just beyond the foot of the stairs?

"Murph, the others are in the cave," Sable told him. "We've got to stop him."

TWENTY-EIGHT

Sable could have kicked herself for sending everyone into the cave. At the time, it had seemed the obvious choice. She reached up and touched the side of Murph's head, where an ugly bruise already mottled the skin. A second concussion within this short of a time frame could be dangerous.

He winced and drew away. "That can wait. I think we need to take the chance that Simmons went into the cave."

"It would be nice to have more firepower," Sable said. "There's a shotgun in the closet where I got this pistol."

"Good idea. I'll stay here and watch."

Sable ran upstairs and grabbed the shotgun, a box of shells and her medical bag, then joined Murph at the basement door. They slipped through the doorway and down the stairs.

No one ambushed them.

At the entrance to the cave, Sable pulled her flashlight out of her pocket, but didn't turn it on. She touched Murph's arm. "We'll have to continue in the dark. Hold on to me, I know the way by feel."

"The pit?"

"I'll stay well away from that."

As soon as they stepped into the black safety of the cave, Sable stopped. "Is that voices, or dripping water?"

"Water," Murph whispered in her ear. "Go on."

They moved deeper into the darkness, groping along the

rough, wet cave wall. They reached the point where the path curved around a column of limestone when they heard a low, angry voice. Simmons.

Sable halted and touched Murph's arm.

"What are you going to do to me?" It was Bryce.

Sable stifled a gasp. No! Simmons was using a child as a hostage! How had this happened?

"You'll be the bait in a nice trap for our friends," Simmons said.

Sable squeezed Murph's arm, urging him behind an outcropping of rock. As he joined her, she saw the dim glow of a shielded flashlight beam as Simmons and Bryce approached.

She waited until Bryce came into sight, walking directly in front of Simmons. She squeezed Murph's arm again. Simmons had the barrel of his pistol against Bryce's right temple. One move could kill the boy.

They could do nothing but watch as darkness descended again, and the footsteps of captive and captor receded.

"Think we should follow them?" Sable asked.

"We can't leave Bryce alone with that maniac, but Simmons isn't taking any chances," Murph said.

"They'll have reached the basement." She started after them.

Murph stopped her. "We can't just barge through the door and say 'boo,' or Simmons's ploy will work."

"But he won't expect us to come at him from the cave."

"Of course he will," Murph said. "Especially once he discovers we're not in the house. Sable, what about that sinkhole Craig found?"

Sable nodded in the darkness. "You read my mind. I left the window cracked in the sewing room, in case we were able to get outside. Once Simmons searches the house, he won't expect anyone to be upstairs. If one of us can get out the sinkhole—"

"I manage better on the ice than you do."

She nudged him deeper into the cave. "We'll see. Anyway, we

need to find that sinkhole, Murph. First, we'll check and make sure the others are well hidden, so Simmons doesn't return and add to his hostages."

Murph was relieved when Sable decided they were far enough away from the house to risk using her flashlight. He was especially worried about Audry and Perry now; Simmons would lose his advantage if anything happened to Bryce, therefore Bryce may be safe as long as everyone else stayed out of the killer's reach.

Sable found Audry and Perry in ten minutes.

"S-Sable?" It was Audry's quavering voice, coming from behind a ledge at the far end of the small cavern of marbled rust formations. The older woman stepped out from behind the ledge, a coil of rope over her shoulder. Perry followed, mud streaking his face, a rip in the right knee of his slacks.

"Oh, Sable, honey," Audry said, "when you didn't show up, we thought that man had you for sure."

"He has Bryce," Sable said.

"No!" Perry exclaimed. "He said he'd be very careful. He just wanted to go back to the basement and listen through the door, to see if you were safe."

"We tried to stop him," Audry said, "but he was gung ho to save you. How do we get Bryce out of that murderer's hands?"

"We have a plan," Murph said, "but it involves keeping the two of you safe."

"I think our best chance is for one of us to return to the house and distract Simmons," Audry said. "That will give the others time to come in and overpower him. I could go."

"He's got a gun." Perry glanced at the medical bag in Sable's hand and at the shotgun Murph had slung over his shoulder. "Are you sure that works?"

"Grandpa kept his guns in good repair," Sable said.

Perry reached behind a stalagmite and pulled out a small shovel. "We hid this back here."

"Good," Sable said. "We need it. Come with us."

"Sable, I've already volunteered to go for help if we can get out of here," Perry told her as he and Audry fell into line behind Sable and Murph. "Don't try to talk me out of it."

"I wouldn't dream of it." She hesitated. "We'll hide you well, but do you want this shotgun?"

"No, you need it more than we do," Perry said.

A few minutes later, breathing heavily, Perry tugged at the collar of his jacket. "It's hot down here."

"That's because you're wearing that heavy jacket," Audry replied. "You thought it would be cold down here, dummy."

"No, I thought it would be cold if we get outside, and who knows when we'll end up outside? That hard ice sure sounds good to me now, and I never thought I'd say that."

Sable stopped in the breakdown cavern, from which two rough passages led. "This is the passage that leads to the sinkhole." She aimed her light along the crawl space littered with smooth rocks from a dry streambed. "This is where we'll come back to get you two. There are plenty of boulders that are great for hiding. You might need to get out of here by yourselves."

"Meaning what?" Audry demanded.

"We need witnesses if something happens," Sable adjusted the rope over Murph's shoulders. "Tell the local police what happened here, and have them check out Otis Boswell of Boswell Mining. I'm sure that's who Simmons works for. The evidence is in the attic safe."

"Do the two of you have only one flashlight?" Murph asked.

"Two, but this is the best one." Perry held up his light. "We won't use the other one unless we have to."

"Good thinking. Don't come out until either Sable or I come back for you…or unless…"

Audry squeezed Murph's arm. "Take care of her."

"I will."

Murph followed Sable silently for several minutes, crawling through tight spots, climbing over ledges, scrambling through a stream. He was grateful for her knowledge of this place, and for her courage.

"I forgot to thank you earlier." He kept his voice low, his gaze trained into the darkness ahead of them.

"For what?"

"For busting me loose when Simmons had the drop on me."

"I did not bust you loose, I merely distracted him."

"If you hadn't been there, I don't know what would've happened."

"The same could be said of you."

"There's just one thing, though," Murph said.

"What's that?"

"In case it ever comes up again, you never warn a killer before you shoot. Just shoot."

She glanced over her shoulder at him. "I'll try to remember that," she said matter-of-factly, shining her light back along the way they had come. "You do realize, don't you, that Simmons might already be back down here?"

Murph nodded. "He'll know by now that we're not in the house."

"But if I have to be trapped in a cave with a killer on the loose," she murmured quietly, "I'm glad it's with you."

"Why?"

"You make a bigger target."

TWENTY-NINE

Sable heard a splash of water, and she grabbed Murph's arm, switching off her light. "Listen."

They stood in absolute darkness and waited for a long moment. She heard only the sounds of their breathing, and the patter of dripping water.

"What was it?" Murph asked.

She turned her light back on. "Probably nothing. Just keep watch behind us."

They were soon walking through drifts of fog that thickened rapidly, reflecting her light back at her. The swirls of mist ebbed and swayed in ghostly patterns, hiding formations that would suddenly appear before them, blocking their path.

They proceeded another fifty yards along the passage, then Murph reached for her light and switched it off.

"Did you hear something?" Sable whispered.

"Water. Listen."

This time the sound of lapping was louder, more definite.

"That's more than just a few drips of seepage," Sable whispered, feeling a stir of excitement. "That's a steady stream. We may have found the sinkhole."

"I think so."

She switched the light back on and they followed the sound of water a few more yards, until icy air and mist as thick as a blanket hit their faces.

"Looks like the place Craig described," Sable said.

"We'll have to climb." Murph pulled out his own light and aimed it all around them, then stepped over to the cave wall and touched it. "Wet. I'll climb to the top, then you hoist the medical bag up to me."

With the shotgun in its sling over his left shoulder, and the Detonics pistol tucked in its holster, he handed Sable his flashlight and climbed the ten-foot bank.

Sable waited until he reached the top, then tossed him the medical bag and flashlight, and followed. They didn't need the shovel, after all. It looked as if Craig had knocked some rocks out of the way.

Murph straightened and stood, placed the shotgun beside him on the ledge and reached down to help Sable the final few feet to the ledge.

He indicated the sinkhole above them, which opened into the night sky with a rough diameter of perhaps two feet. From that opening dangled several long roots from a bush or a small tree.

"If these roots are strong enough," Murph said, "I can use them to pull myself up, then drop the rope down to you."

"Or you could lift me up, and I could tie the rope around the tree or bush that belongs to those roots."

"I'm going first. We don't know where this comes out."

"So what's your point?" Sable asked.

He looked back down at her. "My point is it could be dangerous, I'm bigger than you, so I say who goes." Murph stepped onto the clay embankment. "Hold your light for me, and I'll stick mine in my pocket."

Now was not the time for rebellion. She did as he asked. "Just hurry."

"I'll leave the gun and the bag down here. You can hand them up to me before you come up," Murph said.

"I'll carry the shotgun, Murph."

He reached up for one of the thick roots near the sinkhole, jerked on it, then hoisted himself up, arm muscles bulging as he reached for another root closer to the hole. The root snapped, and he hit the ground with a grunt.

"I liked my plan better," Sable said. "Give me the rope and give me a boost."

Murph readjusted the rope over his shoulder and once more stepped up the slanted clay wall.

This time the roots held. He reached the opening and pulled himself up with a scattering of dirt and pebbles.

A falling rock missed Sable's head by inches and hit the cave floor with an echoing clatter. She turned a fearful gaze back down along the passage, but she saw nothing.

Murph peered back down through the sinkhole. "This comes out by the creek, all right. A couple more feet, and the creek would have been in the cave. The bank is steep and slick."

"So you know where you are?"

"I see a corner of the house from here."

She tossed the medical bag up to him. "Now just tie the rope and get to Craig. I'll sling the gun over my shoulder."

He hesitated, his misgivings obvious on his face in the glow of her flashlight.

"I'm coming, Murph. Just hurry."

Murph withdrew from the mouth of the sinkhole. Seconds later, the rope unfurled beside Sable.

When she reached for it, the beam of her flashlight reflected against a black vein of some kind of deposit in the cave wall a few feet past the sinkhole.

She reached for the shotgun, grasped the rope, then hesitated. With a quick sweep of her light, she found the vein once more. This was no time to inspect further. She had to catch up with Murph.

She turned off her light and stuck it in her back pocket, looped the shotgun sling over her shoulder, then grasped the rope up high and began to climb.

She was halfway to the sinkhole when a light flashed through the mist from the passage below.

She heard breathing, the scattering of loose pebbles, the scuff of shoe leather against hard clay. She held tight, afraid to breathe as the coarse rope bit into her hands and her grip slid. She reached for a better hold. A shower of dirt and pebbles fell noisily across the floor below her.

The light below lit up the mist once again.

She dropped to the cave floor and swung the shotgun from her shoulder, disengaging the safety.

The footsteps neared. The light grew brighter.

She scooted behind a stalagmite as the footsteps quickened. She pressed against the wet stalagmite.

The footsteps stopped. Sable remembered the rope, hanging down through the mist. The beam from a flashlight stopped on it, and then slowly circled the upper cavern.

She held her breath. If she stayed put, she might be shielded by the fog, and it was just possible the stalker would pass by.

She waited as the steps drew nearer. Light penetrated the white mist with an eerie glow, once more illuminating the vein. Sable got a good, close look at it, like a black wire twisting through the rock around it.

Silver turns black when exposed to air….

The footsteps drew closer. She tightened her grip on the shotgun, raised it.

For a moment she was hidden by the glare of the mist. But Simmons stepped around the stalagmite.

He was barely three feet from the barrel of the shotgun. His eyes widened. She pressed her finger against the trigger.

THIRTY

The moonlight bounced against ripples in the creek, so close Murph felt the droplets on his face. Flooding along this creek had obviously caused the erosion of the sinkhole.

After tying the rope securely to the bush he'd used for leverage, he had dropped it back into the cave, then scrambled down toward the water.

Oil lamps still glowed from the windows at the house. Murph studied it to see which window Sable had left open.

Take care of her, Lord. Protect her. He saw the distinct outline of Craig's body in the moonlight.

He glanced back, expecting to see Sable. He didn't. What was taking her so long? He should have insisted she hand him the gun. But one did not force Sable Chamberlin to do anything.

Above the chatter of the creek, he thought he heard a weak moan. He didn't dare turn on his flashlight, but crouched and listened. The moan came again.

"Craig?" he called.

Another moan, mumbled words, then, "Help me…trouble."

Murph glanced toward the sinkhole once more. Sable still hadn't emerged from the cave.

"Murph," Craig called weakly. "That you?"

Murph couldn't wait. He slid down the bank, catching at frozen stubble and rocks to slow his descent. Once out of sight of the house, he switched on his flashlight to find Craig holding his gloved right hand over his heart. Blood stained the glove and glistened from a wound in his chest.

Murph released his hold on a rock and slid the rest of the way down. "I'm here."

Simmons remained frozen in her sights, mist swirling around him, enhanced by the glow of his flashlight. He no longer looked frightened.

Murph hadn't warned her about this—that she wouldn't be able to shoot at point-blank range.

Simmons darted and rushed. She squeezed the trigger. Hard. The gun didn't fire.

Simmons grabbed the shotgun from her and slung it across the cavern as he raised his pistol to her face. "It needs a firing pin. You should have checked for it before you brought it down." He aimed his light at the cave wall. "Looks like you found the treasure. Silver, is it?"

"You took the map from the attic."

"Nope, but it doesn't matter right now, does it? A fella can't mine something from someone else's property. Not until that property's his." He stuck the flashlight into his rear pocket so that the beam reflected from the ceiling, muting the cavern glow. He patted Sable down, and found the pistol she'd stuck into her waistband. She was weaponless.

"Let's go," he said. "Any sudden moves, and I'll shoot you in the head and find what I need some other way."

"Others safe?" Craig asked.

Murph unzipped Craig's coveralls, reassuring the man without answering him directly.

The bullet wound was high on the left side of Craig's chest. With Sable's stethoscope, Murph listened to Craig's breathing. As he'd feared, the bullet had collapsed the lung, but Craig was talking, so his airway was clear. His heart rate was a little fast, and his blood pressure wasn't too bad; he hadn't lost too much blood.

"Craig, I'm going to roll you over and see if there's an exit wound on your back."

There wasn't.

"Is it bad?" Craig asked.

"Not as bad as it could be. You must have started to turn away when he fired so the shot didn't enter straight on. That, plus the heavy coveralls gave you some protection."

"I'll live?"

"You will if I have anything to do with it." He rolled Craig back over. "I'm going to place a pressure bandage over the wound. It's going to hurt, so brace yourself. You might have a broken rib or two from the impact of that bullet."

He placed four-by-four gauze pads on the wound and anchored them with the Elastoplast strips. Craig groaned but didn't complain.

"Now, this is going to hurt," Murph said. "I've got to get you to the house. Just hang on."

"Sable okay?"

"You know Sable, she can hold her own. Now let's go."

Sable and Simmons were nearing the cavern where Audry and Perry were hidden. Sable had to do something fast to warn them.

"Why did you kill Jerri?" she asked.

He shoved her forward roughly. "Just keep walking."

"Why did you try to kill me the night we arrived?"

"I didn't."

"You're not the one who pushed me?"

"I didn't say that, I said I didn't try to kill you. Paul Murphy moved."

"You were trying to kill Murph?"

"Shut up and walk."

For a moment, she just placed one foot in front of the other, but she couldn't resist a comment. "If someone had pulled me from an icy creek, restarted my heart, breathed life into my lungs, I'd have second thoughts about killing again."

"You might," he said. "But you're not me."

* * *

Murph crouched in the sewing room beside Craig, barely daring to breathe. His respect for the overgrown kid had increased as Craig managed not to cry out as he was dragged and carried over the ice and up to the second story window.

Now, if only Dillon didn't bark and give them away. For all Murph knew, Simmons wasn't in the house, but he couldn't risk it.

"Craig, I've got to get you to a hospital soon."

"Can't," Craig said. "Got to help the others."

"I know."

"The…man's crazy…don't let him get away with this." Craig struggled to get up, but fell weakly back against the sewing counter. "And get Boswell. You have a gun?"

"Sure do." He eased Craig against the wall. "Lie still until I can get you to some help. Keep your feet up."

"I'm…not going anywhere."

Murph rechecked Craig's vitals. Little change. "I'll get you out of here as soon as possible," he promised.

He went swiftly through the room, pausing only when he landed on a squeaky board. He stepped past Perry's open case, stopped and aimed his light inside. Cookbooks. He reached down and picked up the thickest of the set. Too light. He replaced the book, selected a heavier one and hurried into the hallway, listening for the slightest movement downstairs.

He desperately needed to backtrack and find Sable, but then he heard Bryce's voice.

Murph rushed to the landing at the top of the stairs and peered over the railing. Bryce was facedown in front of the hearth, looking like a securely tied calf at a rodeo. Next to him stood Dillon. Bryce was talking to him.

Murph gauged the weight of the book in his hand. He descended the first step on the staircase, taking care to place his feet on the outer edges of the steps to reduce the possibility of creaks that would give him away.

Dillon saw him immediately from his perch near Bryce. The dog wagged his tail and whined.

Bryce struggled within the confines of the cord that held him until he could turn his head enough to glimpse Murph.

"Murph!" he said. "Hurry! Simmons is down in the cave."

Flooded with relief, Murph rushed to the boy, dropping the cookbook on the sofa.

"I've got to hurry back down," he said as he fumbled with the cord at Bryce's wrists. This night was not over yet.

Sable knew her landmarks well. It wasn't much farther to the house from here, and Murph could be anywhere. Simmons held her arm loosely enough for her to pull away if she wanted to— if only he didn't have his finger on the trigger of that gun.

A low growl from up ahead stopped Simmons. Sable felt a sudden rush of joy and relief.

"Who's there?" Simmons demanded.

"It's my dog," she said. "He probably followed you down here."

"I closed the door behind me," he said.

"That door won't stay closed. Remember the ghost stories Craig and I told?" She didn't mention that Dillon would never come into the cave alone or with strangers. "Here, Dillon."

The growl ceased. Dillon trotted from the shadows, wagging his tail. Sable reached for him, but Simmons yanked her back.

Dillon snarled.

"No, Dillon." Sable peered into the dark crevices behind the dog.

Simmons thrust her forward. "Get to the house."

As he stepped up behind her, something moved beside them, a quiet rustle of clothing and footsteps on the hard clay. Something struck Simmons in the side. He grunted and fell sideways. Sable yanked from his grasp, swung around and jerked her knee upward—perfect shot.

He buckled forward with a cry of pain.

Sable dropped to the ground and rolled out of his reach, her flashlight clattering on the rocks a few feet away.

The blast of a gun reverberated through the cave. Sable scrambled through the blackness and dived behind a rock as Simmons turned his light back on.

His footsteps came toward her. She lay praying silently for whoever had hit Simmons once to hit him again. Was it Murph? Where had he gone? She crept more deeply into the shadows.

THIRTY-ONE

Murph slammed into Simmons from the side. The gun and the flashlight flew from the man's hand, bouncing off the wall and landing on the ground. The wayward beam gave just enough light for Murph to see him.

Simmons punched Murph in the gut. Murph slugged Simmons in the face. Simmons grunted, stepped back, launched a kick that caught Murph high and hard on the chest, driving the holster and pistol into his sternum, knocking the wind out of him and knocking him to his knees.

Sable cried out. Simmons had grabbed her. Still gasping for breath, Murph struggled to his feet, caught Simmons by the collar of his shirt and wrenched him away from Sable.

Simmons kicked out at her again, wildly, and his foot connected with the flashlight he'd dropped. It flew over the side of the pit and crashed far below.

Darkness. Simmons landed a blow in Murph's solar plexus with his elbow, then jerked away.

Someone shouted to them from somewhere in the cavern. *Bryce.* Dillon barked, then snarled. Simmons cried out.

Murph reached inside his shirt for his pistol. "Sable!"

The darkness retreated as another flashlight came on somewhere in the huge cavern. There was a snap of metal. The wicked glint of a switchblade in Simmons's hand caught the light. He started to lunge forward, but when he saw the pistol in Murph's hand, he stopped and took a step back.

A lightning-quick, muffled ping echoed through the cave. A red starburst spattered across Simmons's chest. He gasped, stumbling backward as shock registered on his face.

The switchblade clattered to the ground. Simmons fell beside it.

Reeling with pain, Murph found Sable in the dim light, rushed to her side and enfolded her in his arms. Breathless and shaking, she collapsed against him.

"It's okay, Sable. I'm here."

"You came," she whispered. "I knew you'd come."

Aching and bruised, he buried his face in her hair, inhaling the sweet scent he'd grown to love as he'd worked beside her, admiring—

"Sable," he whispered, "who shot Simmons?"

Sable raised her head. "I thought you did."

The rumble of Dillon's growl echoed once more through the cavern.

"No," came Bryce's frightened voice from behind the beam of his flashlight. "Dillon, stay back."

Murph's breath stopped. "Bryce, what's wrong?"

There was no answer. Murph helped Sable to her feet and turned to find Bryce standing in the shadow of the ledge, brown eyes wide, his young face frozen in shock.

Beside Bryce stood Perry Chadwick, his high forehead creased in a frown, his thinning hair frazzled across his forehead. The glow of Bryce's flashlight outlined the dark shape of a weapon in Perry's hands.

For a moment, the sight was so incongruous, the impact of it didn't register for Murph.

"Perry?" Sable said. "What's going on? Where did you come from? Is that my gun?"

Dillon's growl rose in a crescendo.

"This, my dear," Perry said, "is a beautifully crafted mini Uzi, complete with silencer. Don't refer to it as a gun."

"But...I don't understand," Sable said. "Bryce isn't—"

"You'd better control your watchdog, Sable, before I'm forced to resort to my own methods." Perry's chubby fingers gripped his weapon with expertise.

"Quiet, Dillon," Murph said.

The dog gave an anxious growl and fell silent.

"Mr. Murphy, drop the toy pistol, would you please?"

Murph had no choice. He complied. The pistol hit the ground with a metallic thud.

"Thank you," Perry said. "Now, Sable, please don't start asking a bunch of silly questions." He spoke as casually as if he'd been sharing stories by the fire. "You know what I want. Do you want to know what happens to Bryce if I don't get it?"

"Let him go, Perry," Murph said. "You're not going to kill an innocent kid."

"He's a teenager. Teenagers are never innocent. They get on my nerves almost as badly as dogs." Perry kept his gaze trained on Sable. "Are you going to give me the evidence your grandfather collected against his poor, long-suffering partner? Don't try to tell me you don't have it. You gave yourself away earlier, remember?"

"Let Bryce go and I'll give it to you," she said.

Perry grimaced. "I need a hostage, and I need those papers, Sable. Now. Don't trifle with me."

"Do it, Sable," Murph told her softly.

"Listen to your boyfriend," Perry taunted. "Don't gamble with this child's life just for a little revenge."

"But I'm not gambling anyone's life, am I?" she said. "You have no intention of letting us go."

"What have you done to Audry?" Murph asked.

"Don't worry, she's hiding in the dark like a good little old lady, waiting for clumsy, heroic Perry to return. I took her flashlight. In case you needed it, of course."

"Let Bryce go, Perry," Murph said. "Take me if you need a hostage."

Perry shook his head. "I'm not quite that bumbling, Mr. Murphy, contrary to the image I have led you to know and trust. Too bad Simmons opted for the old-style, muscle-bound approach to impress our employer. I knew it wouldn't work, though he made an excellent diversion. That just doesn't cut it these days. So much more is demanded now in our profession. Acting... cooking...prospecting for silver. Oh, by the way, Sable, the map was a great help. Thank you for sharing it with me."

"And the watch?" Sable asked.

"If only it had contained a certain series of numbers, it might have saved us a great deal of trouble."

Perry raised the Uzi and took another step, until the barrel of the gun was barely six inches from Bryce's head. "I think we've had enough conversation, don't you?" His voice turned hard. "The papers, Sable. Now."

She turned slowly toward the house. "Those books," she said. "You wanted us to see what was in your case, didn't you? You staged the whole thing, so we'd be too suspicious not to look. You left your case unlocked, even after that big show of outrage about someone searching it."

Perry grinned. "I could've been on the big screen."

"We didn't *open* the books, though," Murph said. "The one I picked up tonight was too light for its size. I expected something heavy enough to throw against the wall as a distraction. Was it hollow?"

"Good job. Cookbooks are boring to most people."

"No wonder you insisted on wearing that heavy jacket down here in the cave," Murph said. "It hid the gun well."

"You knocked me down in the attic, too," Sable said. "You used the window in your room—the sewing room—and climbed over to an attic window. That was why it was so cold when I returned. Did Jerri catch you trying the safe?"

"You can't blame a guy for taking advantage of every opportunity. Did you enjoy my night-vision goggles in the cavern? Don't you just love that ghostly glow?"

Ghost eyes. Murph glanced at Sable, and met her gaze. She hadn't been blinded by the fall, after all.

"Surveillance equipment?" Sable asked.

"Only the best."

"You were in my room, placing that equipment. That's how you knew about the silver."

Perry smiled. "This conversation is terribly interesting, I'm sure, but if you don't stop stalling, I'll be forced to blast our young friend's head to bits." A sudden harshness in his voice gave a chilling emphasis to his words.

He walked them to the low ledge above the cave mouth. "You go first, Sable. Murph, you're next."

Sable attempted to convey reassurance to Bryce with a nod, then turned and knelt to crawl into the basement. Murph joined her, followed by Bryce and Perry, whose aim never wavered. There was no awkwardness in his movements. He straightened and brushed at his clothes with his free hand.

As Sable turned toward the basement steps, Murph caught her arm and squeezed. She frowned and looked up at him. He squeezed again.

A flash of white caught her attention from the mouth of the cave. For a second, the cave's ghost had never seemed more real. But this ghost was actually a very angry woman in her late sixties, wearing a white sweater and black slacks.

"Okay, Perry," Sable said quickly. "I'll take you to the attic and give you the papers you need, but why don't we work out a deal." She continued to talk to cover the sound of Audry's movements. "If you're going to disappear anyway, one of Boswell's unseen minions, you could give us a fighting chance."

"And how would I do that?"

"You can start by handing over that ugly-looking gun of yours," Audry said from behind Perry.

Perry froze, eyes narrowing.

"And before you make a wrong move," Audry said, "let me just mention that I have Murph's pistol—and Sable's, just for good measure. Don't think I don't know how to use a pistol, either. I taught classes in gun safety for ten years."

She stepped into his line of sight. "So. You kill Bryce, you die. It's as simple as that." The click of a safety release reinforced

Audry's words. "There were a lot of things I didn't notice about you until you left me back there in the dark…or so you thought."

Sable remembered the penlight Audry had used on the bus the night of the wreck. She always carried it with her.

A look of iron-hard anger flashed across Perry's face, then was camouflaged once again behind his bland expression. "I should have known, Audry. You are a woman of many talents. However, I can still cook better than you."

Audry stepped forward and pressed the barrel of the Detonics against Perry's neck. "What am I going to have to do to make you drop that gun?"

He continued to aim the Uzi at Bryce for another long, agonizing moment, then sighed and lowered his arm. The Uzi fell from his hand with a heavy thud. "Don't shoot, Audry. I'm not that desperate."

Murph snatched the weapon from the ground.

Audry stepped aside to allow Perry to precede her to the basement steps. "Don't try anything, Mr. Chadwick. My reaction time won me a couple of awards in shooting contests not too many years ago."

"We've got to get Craig to a doctor," Murph said. "Simmons shot him. I think the Jeep is ready to go. I'll do a little more chopping on the bridge before we cross it. I don't want to take any chances on the ice, especially now that we've come this far." He glanced at Sable. "I'm driving."

She shook her head. "I'm driving."

THIRTY-TWO

Sable grinned at Murph in the rearview mirror as she cautiously maneuvered Craig's Jeep onto the highway and turned toward Cassville. Murph was huddled in the back of the vehicle with Perry, who was trussed like a Christmas turkey. Audry sat in the backseat, with Craig's head on her lap. Bryce sat beside Sable in the passenger seat.

"Now, what's Otis Boswell up to this time?" Audry asked.

On the drive to Cassville, Sable filled Audry in on the details.

When they reached town, Sable took Craig, Audry and Bryce to the hospital, then drove three blocks to the police station to deliver Perry Chadwick. Sable and Murph told the police their story and promised to stay around for more questioning. The police would have to contact the Missouri Special Crimes Unit to investigate the deaths.

The FBI was already on the way to pick up Otis Boswell in Oklahoma. It looked as if Perry would be more than willing to testify against his boss to try to save himself, and the evidence Grandpa had left in the safe would be enough to incarcerate Boswell for many long years.

Sable and Murph stepped outside into the quiet, frozen night for a break.

Murph drew Sable close, and she nestled against him. The warmth of his arm chased away the cold and generated its own kind of comfort. She felt at home there, close by his side, protected and warm.

A car whispered by on the road, its headlights turning the limbs of nearby trees into prism reflections. A limb crashed somewhere in the shadows.

Sable shivered. "This is such a fragile world," she said. "Everything is breakable—the trees, the road, the people. Especially the people. I feel as if it could all break into a thousand fragments at the slightest movement."

"It won't." Murph's voice was strong and substantial beside her, resonating in her heart. "God's creation is more resilient than that. People change, God doesn't."

"It's going to take a while to learn to depend on that."

"It'll take your whole life," Murph said. "God works through time to make it just right."

"I wish I had your spiritual confidence," she whispered.

"You're kidding, right? I'm the one who keeps trying to rely on my own strength. You said it yourself. My macho side keeps trying to take over."

She took a deep breath, watching the reflection of lights that outlined the tree limbs. "I guess we'll both learn, given more time. Meanwhile, I could sure use some encouragement."

"In what way?"

"Oh, a strong friend nearby, who can remind me of God's faithfulness, and who can pray with me…you know…pull me out of the deep places, and help me dodge bullets…stuff like that." She fell silent. Was she being too presumptuous?

"How about that private practice you wanted to build?" Murph asked. "Are you still interested?"

"Of course. It's been a dream of mine for years."

"Have you considered sharing the load?"

She looked up into his eyes, and understood what he meant, and was overjoyed.

He reached for her hand and brought it up to his lips. Her skin tingled at his touch. "I think if the two of us have a practice together, we won't starve."

"That would mean you plan to get your medical license."

He nodded. "It's time."

"A small-town practice is not a pathway to riches."

"My biggest concern is staying near you." His arm tightened around her. "I'm not going anywhere," he said, and then he kissed her.

* * * * *

*Watch for Hannah Alexander's exciting
new medical romance suspense series
set at a clinic in fictional River Dance, MO,
starting in January 2008 from Steeple Hill books.*

Dear Reader,

In researching for this book, I experienced some of the excitement of spelunking. Imagine my dismay the day a makeshift ladder broke with me at the bottom of a cave ledge, without a flashlight. My ten-year-old hero, Jason, devised a way to pull me out, utilizing all the rescue equipment in his oversized pack.

It's amazing to experience the total darkness of a cave. Fourteen-year-old Randy convinced me to turn off our flashlights on one expedition, and I will never forget the overpowering darkness.

Have you ever found yourself in a place of such darkness—perhaps not physically, but emotionally?

There is a Hero waiting to utilize everything within His power to light your world. Like my Jason, this Hero is eager to rescue you. Unlike Jason, this Hero has more than a ten-year-old's overstuffed pack. This Hero has all the power of the universe at His command. Try it. Call out through the darkness and see if He doesn't see you through it, in His time, in His power, in His own special way.

Love from

Hannah Alexander

QUESTIONS FOR DISCUSSION

1. When Sable was on the bus as it slid over the icy road, she had to decide whether or not to invite a group of strangers into her home for the duration of the storm. Other than allowing them to continue on and risk death, was there an alternative?

2. Have you ever been forced into a situation to which you were totally opposed? How did you respond? Would you do things differently now if you had the chance?

3. Though Sable worked with Paul Murphy for only six weeks, she trusted him. Are there people you have met in your life whom you automatically trusted? In the end, was that trust warranted?

4. Paul Murphy took a job in Freemont for the sole purpose of investigating his uncle's concerns about the company. At what point did he begin to trust Sable? What do you think convinced him?

5. Sable's grief intensified when she came face to face with her grandfather's past sins. Can you recall a time when a loved one let you down? How did you handle it? Has the relationship been restored?

6. Have failures from your past ever damaged a relationship long after the fact?

7. Sable and Murph both came to a point when they realized it would be possible for them to climb out of the cave to safety, but they chose not to. Why? What would you have done?

8. To what lengths are you willing to go to see justice done? How frustrated are you when an evil person gets away with evil actions?

9. Have you ever read Habakkuk in the Old Testament? Are you comforted by the reminder that God will bring vengeance on the evildoer, or do you find yourself wishing to beat God to it?

10. Murph and Sable both prayed for protection, and yet they knew that protection could come in unexpected ways. Have there been times in your life when you did not receive the protection for which you prayed? Have you come to terms with this?

11. How do you believe Murph and Sable's dilemma would have turned out if they had not depended on God?

12. If Sable and Murph had known the kind of person Simmons was, do you believe they'd have performed CPR when he nearly drowned? Should they have?

13. Was it necessary for Audry to confide in Sable about her past affair with Josiah?

14. Do you believe Josiah should have told his wife about the affair? Would you have done so?

15. Do you feel Craig's father was wrong for protecting him from the legal ramifications of his automobile accident years ago? If not, where would you draw the line?

SUSPENSE

RIVETING INSPIRATIONAL ROMANCE

DID HE KILL JOSIE SKERRITT?

Everyone–including the police–suspected Parker Buchanan of murder. But Kate Brooks knew the brooding loner couldn't have done it. And she knew proving his innocence would take all their faith–and fast thinking–combined. Because the real killer was setting them up for a double murder...their own.

Secrets surface when old friends—and foes—get together.

Look for

A Face in the Shadows

by LENORA WORTH

Available May wherever books are sold.

Steeple Hill®

LIS44290

Love Inspired.
HISTORICAL

INSPIRATIONAL HISTORICAL ROMANCE

The long journey across the West ended in sorrow for Dani Baxter, a hopeful mail-order bride. Upon arriving in Colorado, she learned that her intended had died suddenly, leaving three young daughters behind. Her late fiancé's brother Beau Morgan proposed they marry—in name only—for the children's sake. But she wondered if even this lost man could somehow find peace in her loving arms.

Look for

The Bounty Hunter's Bride

by

VICTORIA BYLIN

Available May wherever books are sold.

www.SteepleHill.com

Steeple Hill®

LIH82788

REQUEST YOUR FREE BOOKS!

2 FREE RIVETING INSPIRATIONAL NOVELS
PLUS 2 FREE MYSTERY GIFTS

Love Inspired®
SUSPENSE

YES! Please send me 2 FREE Love Inspired® Suspense novels and my 2 FREE mystery gifts (gifts are worth about $10). After receiving them, if I don't wish to receive any more books, I can return the shipping statement marked "cancel". If I don't cancel, I will receive 4 brand-new novels every month and be billed just $4.24 per book in the U.S. or $4.74 per book in Canada, plus 25¢ shipping and handling per book and applicable taxes, if any*. That's a savings of over 20% off the cover price! I understand that accepting the 2 free books and gifts places me under no obligation to buy anything. I can always return a shipment and cancel at any time. Even if I never buy another book, the two free books and gifts are mine to keep forever.

123 IDN ERXX   323 IDN ERXM

Name _____ (PLEASE PRINT) _____

Address _____ Apt. # _____

City _____ State/Prov. _____ Zip/Postal Code _____

Signature (if under 18, a parent or guardian must sign)

Order online at www.LoveInspiredSuspense.com

Or mail to Steeple Hill Reader Service:

IN U.S.A.: P.O. Box 1867, Buffalo, NY 14240-1867
IN CANADA: P.O. Box 609, Fort Erie, Ontario L2A 5X3

Not valid to current subscribers of Love Inspired Suspense books.

Want to try two free books from another series?
Call 1-800-873-8635 or visit www.morefreebooks.com

* Terms and prices subject to change without notice. N.Y. residents add applicable sales tax. Canadian residents will be charged applicable provincial taxes and GST. This offer is limited to one order per household. All orders subject to approval. Credit or debit balances in a customer's account(s) may be offset by any other outstanding balance owed by or to the customer. Please allow 4 to 6 weeks for delivery. Offer available while quantities last.

Your Privacy: Steeple Hill Books is committed to protecting your privacy. Our Privacy Policy is available online at www.SteepleHill.com or upon request from the Reader Service. From time to time we make our lists of customers available to reputable third parties who may have a product or service of interest to you. If you would prefer we not share your name and address, please check here. ☐

HISTORICAL

INSPIRATIONAL HISTORICAL ROMANCE

The Long Way Home

In the depths of the Depression, young widow Kate Bradshaw was struggling to hold on to the family farm and raise two small children. She had only her faith to sustain her—until the day drifter Hatcher Jones came walking up that long, lonely road. She longed to make him see that all his wandering had brought him home at last.

Look for

The Road to Love

by

LINDA FORD

Available May wherever books are sold.

Steeple Hill®

www.SteepleHill.com

LIH82787

Love Inspired
SUSPENSE

TITLES AVAILABLE NEXT MONTH

Don't miss these four stories in May

DANGER IN A SMALL TOWN by Ginny Aiken
Carolina Justice

Former DEA agent Ethan Rogers is done investigating crimes...until Tess Graver moves into the neighborhood. A sinister force has followed her. Though Ethan tries to stay distant, he's drawn to protect her.

A FACE IN THE SHADOWS by Lenora Worth
Reunion Revelations

The promising friendship between Kate Brooks and Parker Buchanan is threatened when the police begin questioning him about a decade-old murder. Kate believes that Parker is innocent, but her faith may cost her. The real killer is setting them up for a double murder: their own.

BAYOU JUDGMENT by Robin Caroll

Felicia Trahan is overjoyed with her new lease on life. She loves the freedom of working with Pastor Spencer Bertrand and rooming with her friend, Jolie. Then Jolie turns up murdered. Dealing with threats, attacks and Spencer's dark past will take all Felicia's strength–and faith.

DEADLY EXPOSURE by Cara Putman

A night at the theater turns deadly when reporter Dani Richards stumbles into a murder scene. With the killer on her tail, Dani discovers that her ex-boyfriend Caleb Jamison is the only one who can keep her safe.

LISCNM0408